Advance Praise

"Astringent, fuguelike. . . . A knotty, sui generis evocation of mothers' feelings of fear and loss."

—***KIRKUS REVIEWS***

"I don't know anyone who writes like Balsam Karam. She blows me away. Truly one of the most original and extraordinary voices to come out of Scandinavia in . . . forever. You'll realize twenty minutes after you've finished *The Singularity* that you're still sitting there, holding on to it."

—**FREDRIK BACKMAN**, author of *A Man Called Ove: A Novel*

"Lyrical, devastating, and completely original, *The Singularity* is a work of extraordinary vision and heart. Balsam Karam's writing is formally inventive and stylistically breathtaking, and Saskia Vogel's translation does shining justice to its poetic precision and depths."

—**PRETI TANEJA**, author of *Aftermath*

"Balsam Karam writes at the limits of narrative, limning the boundary of loss where 'no space remains between bodies in the singularity.' With a lucid intimacy, Karam braids a story of witness and motherhood that fractures from within only to rebuild memory and home on its own terms. *The Singularity* is a book of conviction, where those who have been made to disappear find light and keep their secrets too."

—**SHAZIA HAFIZ RAMJI**,
author of *Port of Being*

"*The Singularity* by Balsam Karam is a novel about loss and longing—a mother who misses her child, children who miss their mother, and all of those who miss their country as they try to feel the new earth in their new land. A deeply moving work of fiction from a true voice of Scandinavia."

—**SHAHRNUSH PARSIPUR**,
author of *Women Without Men: A Novel of Modern Iran*

THE SINGULARITY

BALSAM KARAM

Translated from the Swedish by Saskia Vogel

Published in 2024 by the Feminist Press
at the City University of New York
The Graduate Center
365 Fifth Avenue, Suite 5406
New York, NY 10016

feministpress.org

First Feminist Press edition 2024

Singulariteten by Balsam Karam was first published in 2021 by Norstedts, Sweden.

This book was made possible thanks to a grant from the New York State Council on the Arts with the support of Governor Kathy Hochul and the New York State Legislature.

SWEDISH ARTSCOUNCIL

This book is supported in part by a grant from the Swedish Arts Council.

The epigraph by Pablo Neruda on page vi is reproduced by permission of University of California Press. *Canto General*, Pablo Neruda, translated by Jack Schmitt, introduced by Roberto González Echevarría, University of California Press, 2011.

First printing January 2024

Cover design by Sara R. Acedo
Text design by Drew Stevens

Library of Congress Cataloging-in-Publication Data
Names: Karam, Balsam, author. | Vogel, Saskia, translator.
Title: The singularity / Balsam Karam ; translated from the Swedish by Saskia Vogel.
Other titles: Singulariteten. English
Description: First Feminist Press edition. | New York City : The Feminist Press at the City University of New York, 2024.
Identifiers: LCCN 2023032906 (print) | LCCN 2023032907 (ebook) | ISBN 9781558611931 (paperback) | ISBN 9781558613034 (ebook)
Subjects: LCGFT: Novels.
Classification: LCC PT9877.21.A725 S5613 2024 (print) | LCC PT9877.21.A725 (ebook) | DDC 839.73/8--dc23/eng/20230718
LC record available at https://lccn.loc.gov/2023032906
LC ebook record available at https://lccn.loc.gov/2023032907

PRINTED IN THE UNITED STATES OF AMERICA

To Mum and Dad,
Alaa, Eman, Tania,
Adel, Jian, Salam.

Perhaps, perhaps oblivion on earth, like a mantle
can develop growth and nourish life
(maybe), like dark humus in the forest.

Perhaps, perhaps man, like a blacksmith, seeks
live coals, the hammering of iron on iron,
without entering the coal's blind cities,
without closing his eyes, not sounding
the depths, waters, minerals, catastrophes.
Perhaps, but my plate's another, my food's distinct:
my eyes didn't come to bite oblivion:
my lips open over all time, and all time,
not just part of time has consumed my hands.

That's why I'll tell you these sorrows I'd like to put aside,
I'll oblige you to live among their burns again,
not to mark time as in a terminal, before departing,
or to beat the earth with our brows,
or to fill our hearts with salt water,
but to set forth knowing, to touch rectitude
with decisions infinitely charged with meaning,
that severity may be a condition of happiness, that
we may thus become invincible.

—*Pablo Neruda,* Canto General

My first-born. All I can remember of her is how she
loved the burned bottom of bread.
—*Toni Morrison,* Beloved

PROLOGUE

Meanwhile elsewhere—just as the light turns green and the cars along a coastline prepare to leave the city towards the half desert and the mountains—more slowly than ever a woman crosses the highway, which, along with the corniche, is all that holds the ocean ever rising at bay.

The woman is alone, searching for her child.

Nothing in her face recalls what once was and if someone shouts her name, she doesn't turn around and say *no* or *stop it* in the language no one here understands or wants anything to do with; if they stop, she doesn't meet their gaze and if they say wait, she doesn't come back with a *why* nor later *I have just as much right to walk here as you do, why can't you understand that?*

It's Friday and soon the city almost dissolved by the heat will fill up with tourists dressed in bright clothes and on a ramble through the food markets with fried fish and oysters. From the large galleria, the tourists as if from out of a hole will make their way to the museum quarter and the souvenir shops and afterwards, once they've finished shopping, move on to the rose garden, the university and the bookshops, to the corn vendor on the corner by the drooping palm groves, alone in the sun, and the cats in repose, stretching out, waiting for the heat to break and for the sun to set.

Farther on—farthest on where a hill obscures the view and the road muddies in the tracks of digging machines waiting for work to begin—are also abandoned new builds made of pale concrete and steel girders and a small library where only students go.

Yes, right across the road, invisible to those at the university looking out across the green space and the faculties, stand the new builds half-finished, missing most of the walls to what could have been a living room or bedroom, a bathroom, kitchen or storeroom, and that now gaping mostly keep the students shielded from wind and rain.

At night the students roll out their bedding on the concrete and each pushes their one bag all they have left against the wall, dozes off beside it. Then they wake to the sun and the morning haze and lug their bags across the muddy earth up to their department, cast a look around. At this time of day no one but the cleaners walks the empty corridors and no cafés are open with discounted tea, coffee and yesterday's sandwiches; none of the guards asks where you're from or what you're doing there and no one plants their backpack on the empty chair beside them, saying sorry this seat is taken. The students wash under their arms and between their legs in the large bathroom at one end of the corridor then take a seat in the armchairs by the door to wait for their first seminar, falling asleep and sleeping long.

Later they'll meet up around the fire and go over how best to make this unfinished building a home—they'll discuss which walls are essential and from where they'll get the sheet metal and who among them is best at construction and where they can get hold of screws and drills. The students will talk and laugh and before bedtime open their bag and repack it, take out dry socks and a sweater and walk with their flashlight and books in hand up to their spot by the wall.

It's Friday a late summer afternoon and soon the beach now vacant will have litter spread across its sun chairs and parasol stands as the ocean draws back from the rocks and reeds;

the ice-cream vendors will shove their broken carts up the hill past the palms and grill kiosks, and the taxi drivers will run a rag over the seats and the cracked windshields, will wait for men in suits to wave them down and with someone beside them ask to be driven away from the corniche. Soon, the tourists—just as they for safety's sake place a hand over their handbags and keep an eye out for the children who while waiting for work on the beach have fallen asleep sack and rake in hand—will climb the wide pavement along the twilight-bright corniche and the ocean view beyond words for those who can afford dinner and a little wine at one of the restaurants there. The tourists will take a seat and ask for sparkling water and maybe a large bottle of house wine, marinated olives with capers and garlic and salted nuts to tide them over, reclining with the late summer sea in minor revolt and the sky pitch dark and dull above the soon over-encumbered corniche.

The woman searching for her child has been there, she knows what the corniche looks like, and tonight as every other Friday night since her child disappeared she will go back there and wait; she will watch the girls, who appear out of nowhere with a mop and rag in hand, and follow them as they approach fresh spills and polish the floor to a shine once again just as The Missing One did.

She will search and look around the corniche.

Slowly endlessly tired she will wander up there—determined and clutching her bag like it's the most valuable thing she owns, she will sit on one of the benches outside the restaurant where her child was working soon before she went missing and keep the knife warm by passing it between her hands on the corniche.

It's the corniche she thinks of as the traffic light turns green and the shadows deeper than the day before render her invisible; it's the corniche and the girl and the children she sees as she steps out and slowly starts making her way across the road—it's the waiters in their black trousers black shoes and the men with their glasses of beer who stop to shout as the children walk by.

Like any other day she means to continue to the square—to the razed lot they call the alley, and on to the place where the greengrocer is already stacking melons, stone fruit and the coriander The Missing One always wanted to bring home—but she can no longer move, is stock-still in the middle of the road.

Today the world feels different somehow new and if she squeezes her wounds round and open, it doesn't matter if the pus seeps out yellow thick and if she loses her headscarf at the roadside where she in her tiredness has lain down to sleep, it doesn't matter if she gets it back—the air is both replete and empty and just as the woman perceives this she also senses The Missing One's presence and perhaps her smell across the road.

If she stands here long enough—if she stands among the cars, eyes and hands tightly shut in a prayer so intimate nothing but her wish pushes through—maybe the God who proffered but then took back this child will return it to her.

If she prays loudly enough *dear God* as the shouts from the cars resound and the great sun keeps burning unbounded *I pray to you with all I have* maybe something will happen that couldn't have happened before.

If she puts words to the unthinkable *of all my children* as she falls to her knees on the asphalt *she was the one I loved most* maybe something beyond comprehension can come to pass and the child will appear as if in a dream.

She waits, why doesn't the dream manifest?

In the heat her knees stick to the ground and go numb; alongside her the traffic slows to a crawl, then moves on.

In the cars children sit up and watch the woman—across her chest the shirt is gossamer and along her back a tear running down from one shoulder, her body already fading in the late summer heat and across her pant leg dried blood in black stains from thigh to ankle and out to her toes blue and swollen. She seems unfazed by the people who want her to move along, and when she turns around and fixes her gaze somewhere, it is as though she still sees nothing of this world.

Is she going to get run over, their children ask, is she going to die here on the road, they ask, and their parents say, I don't know, maybe she will, and turn away.

In the bag are the same flyers as always, and across her slippers worn ragged by the streets, the same broken straps that rub the back of her foot red then fall off—around her neck one of the girl's shawls darker with each passing day and in her pocket the knife she carries with her wherever she goes in the city.

Later when the slippers no longer hold, she'll walk barefoot to the corniche and the restaurants and up to the railing; later, when no one is looking, she will climb up and over to the sea- and sky-darkened cliffs.

Today something is different somehow stillborn and the woman feels it as she pounds her fists on the hood of the car that comes closest to her and presses a flyer to its windshield:

> *Has anyone seen my daughter? 17 years old, missing since dawn on 1 May. Help me find her, help me get justice.*

She wedges the flyer under the windshield wipers and doesn't turn around when the driver calls her back, doesn't care if he spits and doesn't go back to hit him when he shouts that she is a slum rat, dirt.

She just keeps moving on and when later that same night she stops searching, hands and forehead bloody, you are standing nearby, looking out over the ocean. You don't see the blood, you only see the woman, and soon thereafter the woman throwing herself off.

Late summer one Friday night in a city half obscured by skyscrapers, and half left to the desert and the near-saturated yellow that rolls in and lays itself upon the streets and lawns like a hand, the cigarette vendors dust off their carts though nothing helps but rain, and in the bushes that frame the parks from north to south, something pale green unfurls where once were flowers and red berries to be sucked on and spat out.

This is a place you haven't been before even though you've often wanted to visit, and when you finally walk these streets it's as a tourist, no matter how many times you speak the language that you've known since childhood or ask the hotel staff how it's going, picking up a newspaper where you slowly get up to speed and then relay what you've read to your co-workers within earshot.

On the corniche rises the buzz of men in suits with a woman at their side and along the main road rose vendors wait all in a row; you have strayed from your co-workers to get a little air—*baby needs a walk* you said with your hand on your belly—and when you pass the entrance to the restaurant, the children draw near and greet you; they ask if you'd like to buy the bracelet they're holding out or would you prefer a pot holder crocheted with yarn and bottle caps? You crouch down to get a better look at the children, answering *yes* and *thank you* and putting the bracelet on and the pot holder in your bag. You give them the banknotes you've taken out, then continue across the corniche.

As you turn to face the sky and the sea a single unbounded darkness you spot her.

The woman is standing on the other side of the railing body bent forward almost one with the cliffs and the sea, looking out to where no horizon and no moon makes itself known; when she turns around and looks at or past you, you follow her gaze along the large road over to the grill kiosks and jewellery vendors and see, as she does, the streetlamps white and yellow down by the harbour and the beach.

It's cooling down—you can feel it and so does the woman standing there with her shirt wide open, letting the ocean breeze beat against her bare chest and the bleeding cuts across her stomach; she wants to kick off her pants but doesn't know how, to pull the girl's shawl tighter around her neck even though she can't.

From this night on the children she has left behind in her search for The Missing One, the children to whom she has never quite returned, will sleep closer together and curled up more tightly and above them in the day the sun will by turns be blinding or cold and white—she knows this.

She knows that the water from the bathroom taps will wane and stay cold the whole winter through and their paraffin lamp will more frequently be blown out by the wind in the alley; she knows that the blankets with their tears small and large will no longer keep them warm and the palm fronds the children fill their arms with across the road won't have a chance to dry in the damp and fog that arrive in autumn like a steady rain.

Not before the morning, when the sun again hits the walls and the roofs and sweeps across the children's feet numbed and blue, will the children let go of each other and once again begin to make their way out of and away from the alley; only after the light as white and unbearable as before bears down on the earth and on the children's bodies—awaiting that which will never return—will the children strike out and slowly wander off, leaving that alley.

I hope the woman thinks as her hands clutch the railing more tightly and she sees the sky and sea, a single vast home to which she longs to return—*I hope the children will one day take the other children's hands and go elsewhere* she says and starts listing the names of her remaining children so the sky and sea won't forget them like they forgot and abandoned The Missing One.

Take care of my Pearl and teach her to ride a bike properly she says as her foot skids on the rocks—*let Minna learn everything about the stars and galaxies—she likes that—and give Mo a hard ball that no one else has yet had the chance to kick* the woman says and falls silent.

That's all—that's all she hopes for before you see her throw herself off and then nothing more—then only the dark of night and the sea breeze and the bars and the food, then you and the child in your belly and the woman's bag left on one of the benches white-painted and worn, placed where the ocean view is hidden by the restaurants enormous along the corniche.

Later you take it—you take the bag with you and give the waiters one of the flyers you find, but keep the soap a stump at most from the depths of her bag; you show them the picture of the girl wearing shorts and a sweater and turn around, you don't wave goodbye and don't say *okay* when your co-workers call out, Good night, see you tomorrow, take care now.

In the hospital bed you will try to remember if on that night you were tired or happy and if you were wearing the green or black velvet dress you'd packed; you'll try to remember if you felt the child kicking as you stood for what felt like an eternity on the corniche and if the woman was tall or short, if her hair was the same colour as yours and if it was on you that she fixed her gaze when she turned around and saw the many tourists, made up of people like you, ever flowing back and forth, as if the lot of you were one with the strip of bars bright and the streetlamps ornate along the corniche.

When the woman lets go and slams against the rocks once then twice, it is neither quieter nor more solemn than usual—this at least you remember and this you tell the people who later wonder why you're always circling back to the woman and the corniche. The light from the restaurants didn't get any less harsh and the music didn't die down—the waiters didn't stop serving aperitifs and small plates of cheese and olives, and along the lookout point the tourists didn't back away, did not leave the corniche; you remember that the rocks were shiny, almost mirrored, and a scream rang out that you later hoped was yours even though you've never been able to scream like that and neither did you understand the point—*I don't have it in me* you say later in the hospital bed and clench your fists two hard rocks, beating your face and chest with all your might.

You'll only remember calling for help, saying you saw a woman fling herself off—*I saw her over there* you'll shout so the whole corniche comes running and when you're surrounded by the diners, you'll point to the place where the black water its softness untold washes over the rocks and once again you'll say *there—see?*

The child was healthy at the check-up only a few days ago, what do you mean there's no heartbeat? you ask one of the two doctors who have followed the nurse in and are now standing in silence in front of the ultrasound image of your dead child. Your stomach is sticky and hard and in the examination room you only have the doctors and the back of the screen to fix your eyes on; outside nothing is as it was and when the doctors search for the words you interrupt them, saying *no* or *what.*

You know the irreversible has already taken place, but your refusal to let two white women with a life that never was nor will be yours rewrite what has happened to your child makes you pull yourself together, makes you stern. *What do you mean there's no heartbeat? What do you mean there's no heartbeat? What do you mean there's no heartbeat?* you ask again and again and are finally drowned out by the one who is saying, I mean that the child has died, it is no longer alive—this is what no heartbeat means, she says and turns to her co-worker.

On the corniche the diners ask if you can remember what the woman looked like and if you're sure she jumped off here, there's no trace? Was she short or tall and was she wearing a dress or pants? Was she white or black, they ask, and were you standing here a long time before it happened?

The tourists in baseball caps and shorts, who like you have been dining and drinking on the corniche, ask if you're sure it was a person you saw, and you will later think that at that moment it was already clear you would soon have a hard time distinguishing a person from the cliffs and the cliffs from the corniche, the railing and yourself.

It was a person—I'm sure of it you say as you pace the hospital corridor waiting for your mother, brother and sister to arrive.

Perhaps in a moment of stillness when no one was speaking to you or shouting that the police were on their way, you saw the body float up to the surface once only to vanish again as if in a dream—could that be?

Perhaps when your gaze was fixed on the space between the cliffs and the sky and you saw the sea foam whipping up in an eternal dance across the rocks the woman floated up as though transparent or only half-born into the world, do you remember if that happened?

Yes, perhaps—when your gaze was fixed for a moment on the place where she in falling made impact, not the first time but the second, and saw the water wash over the rocks—did you think she could have had a few breaths left in her, you weren't sure, what were you to do?

Later you are no longer sure of anything, but it's the woman you think of as you lift your child out of the refrigerated drawer cold and press it to your milk-swollen breasts.

Later you will think that your child also died on the corniche even if it continued to grow and kick for months thereafter.

Yes, there you'll think. In a rift between ocean and sky—the moment you got up in an attempt to avoid your co-workers and find a more peaceful spot on the corniche—you suddenly remembered Rozia and how one afternoon she didn't want to play with you.

It was in the days before you all left, you'd asked her if you could go to the playhouse to draw and sing and she replied that she didn't want to be your friend anymore because you'd taken her hand puppet and anyway you were moving away soon. *I'll give the hand puppet back, Rozia* you said and then *who said we're moving away?*

Later that evening your mother told you that people in military uniforms had stopped by and so it was time to pack.

You did as she said and stuffed your favourite dress and the drawings Rozia had given you into a large bag, and then the woman was standing there as the memory ended and your gaze was again fixed somewhere. She was standing on the other side of the railing and then turned around, looked past you on the corniche.

THE MISSING ONE

1

Friday morning one late summer in a city where the trash from the buildings with balconies facing the corniche is driven to where the palm trees droop and the earth corrodes green and brown; to where the children with palm fronds in their arms stop every day to poke around in the puddles of mud, waiting for the dogs to eventually arrive and tear the trash bags wide open.

The children anticipate the dogs bounding atop the trash pile soon taller than the house along one side of the alley, and then them bounding back down and the mound sinking and spreading out; the children watch muddy water pulsing, filling the pits in the ground and flowing out to the cars and the newspaper stands, the shops, the fountain and the cherry trees too.

The woman searching for her child wakes up in the morning sunburnt and sits up in the sand.

The great loss has already rolled in across the earth, grief and drought, a tattered sunbaked landscape cupped by two empty hands; these days are not the days that once were and this place is a different place, the air close and old, and the city a hole between what came to be and what could have been.

If I feel the sun to be large and hot, it is even hotter to the child she says from her place on the beach, lifting a fistful of sand to her cheek—*if in daytime I always appear as the stranger I am in this city, then the child must also appear somewhere—if only I could find the right position and turn my gaze in her direction* she says, looking around as if seeking the place from which the child might finally appear across the beach.

The inner distances are greater—between memory and memory and from experience to experience time no longer passes, and the woman does not know where she is or why, whether it was a year or a lifetime ago that the child was playing in her belly and the sun almost extinguished was setting over the sugarcane fields and the mountains, or whether she will again be consigned here tonight, to this place on the beach, to the here and now.

She no longer knows whether the homes on that distant hillside existed at all before they, at dawn with the morning haze, were levelled to the ground; nor does she know whether anyone sees her today as she like every other day searches and calls her child's name throughout the city, saying *you are not alone, my beloved* and thinking of the mother among the tent rows who pressed her little bundle already blued against her body and sang the only lullaby she knew in the language she had not yet forgotten.

The mother said *I can hear him breathing* and held out the baby for the people sitting around to inspect, then crawled onto the rug in the middle of the tent and asked *can't you hear it too?* before falling back into her rocking and singing.

I saw it happen with my own eyes the woman says out loud from where she is sitting, the morning waves foaming and the sand dunes before her—*it happened to the woman two tents over* she says *and I could see that nothing of the child remained, but I couldn't say anything to the mother, to the mother I said nothing, for that mother I had no words* she says and stands up.

Today the world feels different somehow new and the woman decides to search for her daughter one last time and thereafter no more—never more by the sea or along the harbour and not by the deserted plots of land or in the half desert below the mountains.

She takes stones from the water's edge and stamps out a rectangle, lets the stones frame a bed and a pillow and says *if she passes by, she will know that this is a resting place* before continuing her daily trek through the city. Today she will first go to the alley, then to the square and the library and finally return here, to the beach and the corniche.

She walks slowly, stopping often, looking around, waiting impatiently in the city.

Sometimes it happens that someone turns to watch her while she is speaking loudly and angrily or softly close to tears, saying *my child* and shutting her eyes or *have you eaten anything today?* as if The Missing One were standing right beside her and could answer once and then again.

Maybe if you wait in the shade of the walnut trees for a barefoot mother to come by and take you in her arms she says and turns around—*maybe if on the street corner by the newspaper stand you feel a familiar eye seek you out and understand that it is me* she says and looks down the road this way and then that.

She sees them—she sees that those who have stopped to look at the dust and the stains, the bag she carries close to her body and the bare feet with split nails and cracked heels do not understand to whom or in which language she is speaking, and so she wants to say *hello* and *wait*, explain herself. The woman wants to share something about her girl with the few words she has managed to commit to memory without them taking fright or turning away, but this too she sees is impossible—they are now speeding their steps up the street to the traffic lights and melding with the swarm that begins on the other side of the road.

What is there if it cannot be close to this and this the woman says and first puts a hand to her belly then to her forehead damp and warm, moving on in the morning sun to the alley.

What is there if it must always be taken away she says and removes her headscarf, wipes her face and the back of her neck, glances up at the sky as blue and blithe, as high and smooth as always, when she makes her way to the children and her mother, all waiting for The Missing One to return to the alley.

Friday morning one late summer in a harbour town spread out along a coastline nestled against the mountains and near a bay that farther up, in another country, curves in and out the image of a half moon, soft and beautiful.

The children in the alley run their hands across the half moon on the map and then draw it in the dust across the sun-drenched alley.

The children say *on the map all mountains look alike, but I know that one is red and by that red mountain we once lived.*

They say *from a hole in the middle of the red mountain ran water soft and pink, and when in the afternoon sun we kicked the ball against the mountain face, the water beaded on our arms and legs and cooled us down, gave us shelter; the water lifted us up high, a cloud of mist to hide in when someone looked up from the road and heard us playing and sleeping and living and eating by the red mountain, do you remember?*

Yes the children reply to each other and say *we followed the water into the ditch and onward between the homes and saw that at the hillside it pooled like a shimmering lake of garbage and mud—this we remember.*

Minna looks up from the half moon drawn in the alley and continues *do you remember that we took fistfuls of that mud and built small beds where the kittens could sleep, and we filled the beds with dry grass and newspaper and later dried flowers, dried palm fronds broken and shredded and some old rags? Do you remember that the kittens liked it better there than anywhere else and we felt that so keenly then, that we had done a good thing?*

Yes Mo and Pearl reply and continue running their fingers in lines across the alley, now drawing the red mountain and the homes they once had and the ditch and the hillside; the children draw the school at the foot of the slope and the awnings that ran between their homes and also the mountain of trash a short distance away; they draw the water tap and the bicycle and finally the kitten beds like a scattering of small dots in the heat soon unbearable in the alley.

It's morning and the sun beats down on every child and every stone fallen from the ruined wall and collected in the middle of the alley; it's morning and the rats zip down the broken waterspout and into the rubble by the house next door, and the cockroaches shimmering find their way out of the dust and climb the walls, going as far as they can away from the alley.

Here there are no longer friends to call out to and no starry sky under the red streetlight's glow, and neither a hillside nor a mountain rising to hold and comfort, to shield the children from the wind and the rain or just from the cars and eyes prying deep into where the children are sleeping and eating and walking and playing in the alley.

The alley is dusty and deep and at the far end, where the sun does not reach and something darker and larger blooms, there a grandmother sits against a wall keeping a watchful eye on the children.

If she comes home tomorrow, I will draw a flower and a house and next to the house I will draw a ditch and above the ditch a haze the children say and search for a piece of paper that blew in and landed in the alley; *if she wants to borrow my catapult, she can have it and if she wants to sing a song, I will sing it, even though I don't know how* the children say and draw the flower, the house and a palm with leaves big enough to keep the rain off.

Grief draws in and widens the distances without the children knowing how or why, and in the bushes that no longer bloom, what is burnt pushes through the deep green and takes over; at the mouth of the alley, an orange tree no longer rises like a crown over the patch of earth where The Missing One would sit with her notebook, and down the road a neighbour no longer stops by to ask the children if they want to come along to the beach or the square for a bit.

Rocks are mountains the children say as they sit either at the ruined wall or in the middle of the alley, waiting for The Missing One to return home.

If you hold a stone in your hand, your hand takes the shape of the stone and if you put the stone in your mouth, your mouth becomes as hard as the stone they say and press their stone hard into their hands.

Yes the children reply—*if you stack your stones, you can build a hut and if you throw your stone at something, the stone will always win* the children say and either pour out or collect the stones that have fallen from the ruined wall in piles across the alley.

Unless it's at water the children say to each other and look up.

Yes, unless it's at water the children reply to each other and look around.

If the loss is present, the children no longer

know whether it is their mother or sister it has laid claim to, and if heads tilted they stand by the ruined wall and search in the swarm across the road, they no longer know which of the two to search for.

Remember when she came home with a big tin of olives and we sat down to eat every single one? the children ask as they lie there and lift a medium-sized stone towards the sun, holding it there and letting it for a moment hide and push away the sun.

Yes, I remember the children reply—*she was happy and cheerful that day, had found a friend there on the corniche and said it was getting better, a girl who worked a few restaurants down and who she could smoke and talk with, they could accompany each other home and maybe she could even invite her here, she said. The olives gave us a stomachache that lasted all night and into the next morning too* the children say and start sorting the stones they've collected in order of size from one side of the alley to the other.

When Mum and Gran came home from the market, we had to keep quiet about it even though we were rolling around in pain the children say and laugh out loud for the first time in a long while in the alley.

But then we teased her when we saw her carrying the pits in a bag and tossing it into the container across the road the children reply and look at all the piles that have now grown bigger and spread across the alley.

It was a heavy bag the children say and take a stone from each of their own piles and put it in their sweater now stretched out and pale from all the stones borne across the alley.

Imagine the people on the corniche got angry when they realized she'd taken the olives even though the can was only going to be thrown away the children say and from the depths of their sweater pile the stones into a mountain in the middle of the alley.

Yes, imagine if that's why she disappeared the children say to each other and use their feet to dig a trench that runs from the mountain to the ruined wall and the road, they build a sort of hillside in the alley.

Mum didn't like her working there the children say and place stones like homes on either side of the ditch and farther away a school, a food storehouse, a small house for the cats to sleep and play in.

No, she was worried and angry and one time they fought and stopped talking to each other for a whole day the children say and line up stones like labyrinths around the homes, building a wall and erecting a shelter.

Then just before she had to go to work Mum hugged and kissed her, told her to be careful, that Friday nights were the worst on the corniche they say and decide that the labyrinths are borders you cannot cross any which way, not without first asking permission and paying a toll.

What if the people on the corniche harmed her the children say to each other, now quieter, and decide that if you crossed a border and grazed a stone, you are not allowed to cross another until you have stuffed your mouth full of stones and said a rhyme out loud in the alley.

She had bruises all over her arms and legs the children reply to each other and decide that the rhyme should be one that Mum had taught in the tent school before the people in military uniforms arrived and took everything the children hadn't had time to carry along with the slate and the table, as well as the map of the world they'd drawn and the shelf Mum got from the nice lady at the library.

Yes, and all over her back and chest too, I saw them when she was washing herself in the bathroom one day and I happened to go in there they say and slowly begin to move through the labyrinths, their mouth full of sharp stones and their rhyme drawn out as the morning sun crosses the alley.

The children play a while and rest a while, position themselves to look out over the road and search for ants near the ruined wall a while. Then they sleep, long.

When they wake up it all begins again and they do what they usually do in the same order and in the same way as before: take out the bread bag from the tin that once held flour and salt and put the part of the bread that hasn't gone mouldy on a newspaper, pour a can of beans on top, and slice some tomato or cucumber and put it on the side.

Sometimes they call for their grandmother to come and sometimes she steps out of the darkness and says *thank you* and *that's enough*, says she can still feel yesterday's bread in her throat and again disappears into what has become her spot at the end of the alley.

Now and then the greengrocer comes by to drop off more cucumbers and more plums, asking if the children have seen their mother lately or if they've had any news about their sister, will she be coming home soon?

The greengrocer asks if they are managing

well in the alley and if Gran is cooking what he's been dropping off, and which out of the corner of his eye he sees is rotting in bags next to the wall. He asks about the men who make their way here—if there are fewer of them now that the tourist season is over—and if the children are sleeping better and no longer having nightmares in the alley.

The children answer *maybe* or *no*, say *we haven't heard anything about our sister and Mum hasn't been here in a long time* and then again *I don't know.*

The greengrocer leaves more bread and beans, and the children thank him and follow him to the ruined wall and the pavement—that's as far as the children will go, and when the greengrocer disappears towards the square, the children think they can see the cherry trees and the library, the food stalls and the fountain; they think they can make out the light that this time of year always hits the shop windows and the playground and also how it thereafter softly falls back on the same cherry trees billowing large by the fountain.

The children see this and turn away.

After eating they rinse their hands and begin again collecting stones collecting scrap, waiting for something anything to happen, and pressing the rocks to their bodies.

What day is it? The children don't know, can't read their way to it, have no one to ask.

Was it recently or long ago that their sister disappeared and is tomorrow the day she will finally return?

Will it be this winter that they start school and are given a home where they can rest and warm themselves, draw and play?

The children look up at the trees and the sky and then turn back to the ruined wall and the alley, pick up a stone.

Late summer, one Friday morning in an alley where no one hangs palm fronds anymore green and speckled, and no one knots two ropes together and jumps rope with the children happy under the shadows of the tarpaulin, stretched like a roof from one side of the alley to the other.

No one tugs at the other's hand anymore and says *come, look what I've found* and no one follows after and laughs, taking a bumblebee more beautiful than ever out into the sun and leaving it on the pavement a short distance from the alley.

The grandmother sits in the dark and looks around.

When construction began on the house next door to the razed lot they call the alley and the walls were torn down in anticipation of new ones for a new house with new windows and new doors, a prettier garden and a metal gate with no bullet holes or dents from the war, it was no longer possible for the tarpaulins to hang across the alley, leaving it bared to the sun and the world.

She tried to hang up the tarpaulins, to protect the children, but it wasn't possible—the walls on one side weren't there anymore and her spot was the only one that still had a stump of wall from which a piece of cloth could be hung to draw a darkness over her deeper than she could ever have imagined and all that had been left for her to take care of in the depths of the alley.

The grandmother went into the darkness and there she stayed.

From here she can see the movement of loss and doesn't know what to do; she sees it all the time and fears it as she sits there watching over the alley—she even sees it when the children for once seem to be laughing or playing, and fears it too in dreams when they emerge from the red streetlight bruised and naked, and tell her yet again that the girl has disappeared.

If I stand in the middle of the road and stay there, even if everyone wants me to keep going she mumbles—*if I rip one of the men out of the driver's seat and threaten to slit his throat, maybe someone will give her back to us* she says almost invisible from the back of the alley.

Have the missing ever returned she says and runs a hand over the wall and the bullet holes sharp in the middle of the wall—*has spilled water ever been unspilled* she says and falls silent.

It is summer, even if the tourists have left the cool cottages in the mountains and the small shops along the promenades have shut their doors; summer, as if summer never wanted to end, and past the broken windows of the deserted houses red dust ripples towards the grass.

It doesn't cool down no matter how many pieces of cloth the grandmother spreads across the ground, not even if at dawn she douses the alley with water from the tap in the only bathroom they dare to enter, with the roof almost split in two and the green tiles in pieces underfoot; the alley will not cool and in the air the swallows fly ever higher and fall again and again against the half-demolished roof of the house.

The grandmother remembers, watching over the children in the daytime and at all other times turned to darkness waiting for those who should return, it's high time now, where are they?

She remembers that once her cousin Naima and later The Missing One were with her and now neither of them is here—her daughter only barely so, returning to the alley only sometimes.

She did what she was supposed to and was loving and held them close—even so neither of them is here, why is that?

Where are they? Why don't they come home?

She wants Naima and The Missing One

back and leaves her spot from time to time, slaps herself hard across the face and thighs and pulls off her headscarf, waving it in the air.

The grandmother picks up the tea glass as if it were hot even though she hasn't boiled tea for days and pretends to eat a piece of bread even though there is no bread at hand. *Would you like some?* she asks The Missing One as if she were sitting beside her, and then *you don't eat enough, you never have, I don't like it. When you get home, I'll throw you a party—I promise this before the stars and God—and I'll take off these ugly black clothes and wear something red or airy, this I swear. I'll wash and comb my hair and offer bread and sugar to anyone who comes walking down the street; I will air the blankets and mattress so you can sleep the softest sleep and I'll cook all your favourite meals even if my hands have forgotten the measurements and I no longer know what you like, can you tell me?*

Do you remember how we used to roast the tomatoes soft over the fire and I would call you in to eat from where you were playing with the other children by the hillside and the mountain face? You'll never grow big if you don't eat, I said, and how you gave no answer even though what we'd prepared was so tasty and sweet and not as hard to get hold of as now—do you remember that?

Do you remember how we were able to bring home what we needed without being beaten up and how bad it got when they started marking us in town? Still you grew taller than all the children running up and down the hillside and taller even than me, no matter how many times I begged you not to grow past me like that. I used to watch you, see how the children gasped when you got up from dinner by the hillside and how afterwards they'd knock on our door and ask you to pull at their hands and legs to make them as tall as you, do you remember that?

I used to look at you and when you turned around, you'd blow me a kiss and I'd blow two or three back.

Do you remember how you'd linger by the ditch for hours waiting for Mum to turn off from the road? She'll be here soon, I said, but you wanted to see her—nothing would do but seeing her with your own eyes coming up the hillside with sacks or planks over her shoulder and then you'd run to me at the same time every day saying Mum's coming, Mum's coming, as if it were a miracle that your very own mother was returning from the sugarcane fields and taking you in her arms each day.

The grandmother fidgets in her pit, puts her hand over her mouth, squats down. She can no longer stand to see the children's movements in the alley and instead stares at the wall.

I was your age when my cousin Naima disappeared and a few weeks later the neighbour girl Selma too, Selma who everyone thought was so bright and beautiful and who I never got to know except for sharing the occasional soft drink and smoking one of the cigarettes she always had with her. I remember that it was winter and I didn't have a warm jacket and the power was always cutting out; I remember that Naima got sad and cried ever more often and that sometimes I'd steal chocolate for her or bring a newspaper from the stand near our home. When she disappeared Mum kept me home from school for weeks and didn't let me go along to the market or visit my aunt and our young cousins who didn't know what to do with themselves amidst waiting for Naima and everyone who was searching for Naima along the roads and in the desert. I was searching too even though I wasn't allowed—setting out when Mum and Gran were in the fields and searching for Naima and Selma where I thought they might be held captive by those men they had talked about and feared. Once I walked all the way to the city centre to wait for a car to approach me as I knew they had approached Naima on her way home from the food storehouse one evening. And as I stood there by the red lights, one of the men slowed down and looked at me, rolled down his window, made a gesture. I ran away as fast as I could and escaped by a hair, can you imagine? the grandmother says and moves in the darkness now deep and resounding across the alley; *I made it out then, my darling, but I ended up here instead* she says and lies face down in the dust, saying nothing more.

2

Morning one late summer in a city where the cargo ships dock for days longer than the cargo demands and the crew, wanting some fun in the evenings, take the back streets from the harbour to the bright and ever visible corniche.

The woman searching for her child stands with her back to the sea and presses her lips to the red star someone has painted over a pull-down grille, eyes shut long into the kiss. Thereafter she continues with her bag slung over her shoulder, down street after street towards the alley, and searches as she goes through the shipping containers and the abandoned parks, the new builds and redevelopments and then the back streets out to the gates of tall buildings she is not allowed to enter.

She has aged, it shows—in her emaciated body nothing is held high anymore and under the headscarf her hair is ever sparser and whiter; all across her arms, rows of yellowed wounds open to the heat, and from the corner of her mouth, a slit as if drawn by a knife from cheek to ear.

She moves all the while as though she were about to fall headlong into that from which she never wants to rise again—she moves always onward. The Missing One must be somewhere, but she is never where the woman is looking at the moment and so she wants to press onward; time and space will never meet above the city and so the woman keeps moving, always away and always onward.

Later she will reach the corniche lit up in the night, its breeze cool and perfumed, and stay there.

She will reach it and this time she will not be shooed away by the waiters rushing between closed parasols and set tables; no, the waiters will not as before ask her to keep away and mind the plates of olives and garlic bread, and she will not listen when they tell her not to touch the cheese boards and crackers, to keep her distance from the tourists hugging their handbags and not to scare away the diners who approach the restaurant, see her and turn right back around.

Neither will the woman care when the waiters warn her against asking yet again to speak with the manager and mentioning that girl; she's not here, they'll say—we haven't seen your daughter in months and if she came here, we'd drive her off, they'll say to the woman with her back turned to the corniche.

I'm searching for my daughter the woman will shout as loudly and clearly as she can—*she worked at this restaurant and it is for her sake that I have come* she will tell the waiters and all those who can no longer carry on as if nothing has happened on the corniche.

When the woman thinks she recognizes a man in a suit from the nights her child was working, she'll shout *hey you, pig,* and when she sees a girl moving in the shadows between the waiters and the kitchen she'll call her by The Missing One's name even if she can see that the girl is someone else with someone else's hair and hands and height, is nothing like The Missing One; the woman will see that the girl has a different back bent over the heavy gas canisters carried across the restaurant floor and that her arms are not as bruised as those of The Missing One; she will see that the girl has a different fear as she smokes by the kitchen entrance and also a wider gaze when she catches sight of the woman, a mother other than the one she had hoped would be standing there to walk her home.

The woman will shout her daughter's name and when no one answers she will turn to face the cluster of children who after working on the beach have wandered up to find something to eat and drink on the corniche.

She will greet them and ask if they have seen or heard any news about The Missing One and the children will say as they've said many times before *I don't know* or *I can't remember.* They will say they haven't seen anyone on these streets tonight and it's hard to know who's who among the missing, there are so many of them nowadays. *Is she older or younger than my friend Amira who disappeared the other week?* the children ask and look across the corniche—*and did she know Simona or Malika?*

I think Simona will be coming home soon the children will say and their gazes will linger on the outdoor dining areas and grill kiosks—*I think Simona's brother said he'd seen her outside a shop in the city and she had taken all the money he was going to use to buy detergent and matches, and she'd told him she'd be home soon, she promised* the children say and move towards where the food is being served on the corniche.

What did you say she looked like? the children ask, holding a sandwich from the nearby grill kiosk, and the woman says *tall and attractive, black clothes and short hair* and gestures with her hand to show how her hair only went to here.

The children have a think, then shake their heads and say *no, her I haven't seen, but have you looked by the harbour? After my older sister disappeared, she was found in a locked building in the harbour* says one of the children as she keeps pulling her younger sibling away from the railing and the white tourist couple, who in their shorts and linen shirts have turned around to watch them from their spot at the railing.

Only after did we find out that she hadn't been allowed to leave even though she wanted to the child continues with a tight grip on her younger sibling's hand—*she had screamed and shouted for help many times and then one day when they forgot to lock up she was able to run home* she says and finally follows a bit closer behind her younger sibling by the railing, watching the sea large and black, an eternity straight down.

The woman plants herself between the children and the white tourist couple and says *okay, I'll search the harbour one more time* even though she knows it's not true because her search ends tonight.

The woman sometimes has it in her to muster a smile or to embrace the children who have followed the stream of tourists up to the corniche for bread, soft drinks and grilled chicken. She sometimes tells them *this is how you slap away an arm if he comes at you from behind* or *this is how you keep the wounds on your knees clean and dry*; she sometimes has it in her to say *I noticed that the yellow cat on the boardwalk has had kittens, have you seen them?* or *when I was little we used to dry flowers under hot stones in the sun*, but for the most part she just turns away and doesn't listen to everything they're saying and their repeated requests for help, *can you please do something?*

The woman doesn't answer when the children ask if she knows of a warmer place to sleep now that the cold is rolling in or if she can have a word with the waiters at the corniche. *We need money for food and now that my sister can't work anymore it's my turn* the girl says more seriously than ever. *If you have a chat with them, maybe I'll get to work here even though I'm not old enough* says the girl—*please, if you tell them you are my mother and you're fine with me being a cleaner at this restaurant, maybe they'll let me do it* she says and takes the woman's hand.

It's Friday and the morning sun is as high as before and the woman keeps thinking to herself that tonight she will not be forced to leave the corniche—she is sure of this as she sits near the alley and in her mind slits the throat of the restaurant manager and slaps away the young hands outstretched.

Here no one knows how I used to wear my children like a crown the woman says and looks out over the pavement—*in this city no one has seen me write words on the slate and listen to the children as in loud voices they let the written word resound in the room* she says and falls silent. The woman pulls off her headscarf and wipes her face, presses the bag with the photos of her child harder to her belly and covers her mouth with her hand.

If the loss is present, it has for as long as she can remember been inside her and she says *do you remember when the homes were demolished?* as if addressing someone by her side and then *I thought that was the worst thing I'd ever have to experience. Stuffed into trucks like cattle and scattered across different parts of the country so as never to be able to build a common home again, I didn't think it could get any worse* she says and presses her headscarf to her face—*but here I am, God* she says—*here I am.*

Can traumas be ranked? the woman then screams out loud, not knowing why she's screaming.

Can they? she repeats now much more quietly and looks around, her gaze lingering on a boy standing by his moped, who looks back at her. She raises her hand in greeting and tries as best she can to find the words she hasn't had time to learn so he won't walk away in fright. The woman says *nice one* and points to the moped, says *my boy would like it* and then *very nice* as clearly as she can before the boy turns his back and continues working on the moped.

If the loss without end is present—and it is, she can feel it like she can feel her fingertips on her eyelids and the dust that sometimes sweeps along the street and disappears—it has been inside her as far back as she can remember.

If you knew our homes were going to be demolished, why did you let us build them? If you knew that one morning they would come and take everything away, why didn't you let the mountain rise up and give us shelter?

From here she sees the alley like a shadow between two damaged houses, ramshackle since the war, or an offshoot from the motorway leading into nothingness. She knows that the alley is now more a state than a place and so moves more slowly the closer she comes, stopping from time to time, looking for someone to walk with and then waiting eyes fixed on the opening to the alley.

Yes, from here she can hear her children's voices rising in fractured sentences and in rhyme and sees the old orange tree now no more than a trunk broken and bent over the alley—she sees the ruined wall lower than ever and also the darkness at the end of the alley.

One Friday morning in the city where cars big and white are parked along small streets and carts knock them dented and dull, yet another mound of trash grows larger with all that no one knows what to do with anymore.

At the end of the day the men walk up to their cars, run their hands over the new dent nearest the headlight and search the street; the men search as if they now might run into the responsible bread or juice vendor, and before they drive away as they do every day, they approach the cigarette vendor across the street and ask if he has seen anything. My car got bashed, the men say—did you see who did it? they ask, still wearing their sunglasses.

The cigarette vendor shakes his head and then goes back to reading his newspaper.

The children see the white cars driving and sometimes sit down to count them, up to sixty or seventy before they tire and again shut their eyes in the morning sun vast across the alley.

Here is the slowness and the endless heat, the trash blown in and left behind and the children's increasingly emaciated bodies, their small repeated movements across the alley; here is the dust and the drought, but no longer the smell of laundry hanging from lines so low the children must duck under, and neither a friendly pat nor a song to sing to pass the time; along the walls there are no longer bowls of washed rice or yellowed paper for the children to paint, nor is there a ball to kick or a pasture drawn on the faded squares laid across the alley.

As if the world were at a standstill and the days one and the same, the children sit open to the road and see all the passersby and how they observe them defeated as if in solitude or just anticipation in the alley.

The children no longer shield themselves when someone points at them and says something they don't understand; they don't turn away, don't cover their face with a hand and don't hide their wounds, small swollen lines across their legs, when an observer continues down the pavement, leaving them as they were in the alley.

The children no longer call out *Gran, I'm thirsty* or *there's a rat at the ruined wall, what are we going to do about it?* nor search the containers for flour and sugar and tea and coffee; they no longer collect the dregs of cooking oil at the bottom of glass bottles that haven't yet broken; they hang no herbs to dry, keep nothing cold in a shade that no longer exists and do not sweep the dust out of the alley.

Once she came with me to the square to pick flowers for Gran's birthday and on the way home we saw a kitten in the bushes under the palms. It was love at first sight and when I bent down to pet it an old man shouted from a balcony, said I wasn't allowed and should leave at once. I remember how angry this made her and how she shouted something at the old man the children say. *Then she picked up the kitten so I could cuddle it and when we were done we went back home* the children say and toss a stone high in the air in the alley.

Yes, and another time she took me to the sea after we'd been selling washcloths at the market and once we'd finished swimming she said we were going to the corniche for ice cream and we both chose chocolate and when the people on the corniche saw us with our ice cream they called her over, but she was off that day so she said no and we didn't go there and instead we came back home the children say in the alley.

The children don't pick up cans to throw at the observers' heads anymore so no one laughs when they miss or cheers for each bullseye; the children no longer pull back their slingshot or sling their stones and sing none of the songs they were taught as the mist above the metal roofs and the mountains eased and they assembled at the hillside to watch the starry skies more beautiful than ever.

Back then The Missing One would sometimes arrive at the hillside later, when everyone was already sitting with tea and bread and fruit and butter, waiting for the starry sky and the moon to appear; it happened, and just as she lay down tall and large among the children, they asked her if she had been in the schoolhouse arranging again. *Have you? Have you been in the schoolhouse doing that thing you never tell us about?* Minna asked and looked at her sister and at her sister's hands and then *but what are you actually doing there?* as the blue of the heavens drew away and a new moon rose and *can we come with you next time?* at the very moment the mothers switched off the electricity powering the generator and the lantern went out and the whole hillside looked up at Orion and Virgo and the Little Dipper and the Plow.

The children play for a long time with the mountain and the homes and the labyrinths and the borders in the alley, and when the stones in their mouth draw blood they take a break. They take a seat at the ruined wall with the yarn no one crochets anymore and plait the strands into long snakes to toss out then pull back, waiting for something anything to happen, shutting their eyes to the dust and light across the alley.

The children no longer know whether it is today or tomorrow that their mother will return holding their sister's hand in hers, nor whether it was yesterday or a year ago that they were driven here with what little they were allowed to keep wrapped in blankets and sheets, a skirt large enough to carry pots and pans in and two big sacks they later tore open and placed on the ground as a buffer to the cold in the alley.

The children don't know if long ago they ran back and forth to the tent school and carried as many books as they could get their hands on before it was levelled to the ground, nor whether now is when they must once more line up before the people in military uniforms and with their mouths open wide feel those thick fingers searching their throats.

They no longer know whether it was before or after the people in military uniforms broke the water tap in two and pulled up the berry bushes and took away the lantern, nor whether it was at this moment or later that they filled the ditch with the demolished walls and tossed the tarpaulins in a pile beside.

Was it yesterday or a lifetime ago that they were instructed to stay here and wait like others have had to wait, for months perhaps years, and is it tomorrow that they will yet again be paid a visit by the relief organization that says hello and how are you all then here you go and we'll be back soon, even if it's not true?

The children don't know, don't remember, have no one to ask.

If you make a paper airplane, I can fly it over the ruined wall and the road the children say to each other and hold out a piece of newspaper that has blown into the alley—*if you shut your eyes tight and count to ten* the children reply and turn their ears tense to the ruined wall and the road.

Will someone finally find their way here and will they come into the alley?

Will they say they've bumped into the sister along the corniche or seen Mum sitting at the far end of the harbour, and will that person try to get the children to go there with them? Will the children rise from the dust and disappear and will someone search for them after they go?

Does anyone ever come here these days and if so, who? The children wait and listen, as usual barely moving in the alley.

Morning, cars in motion towards the beach and inside the alley nothing—only the children scattered like little flat stains along the ruined wall and the ground and then nothing.

The grandmother leaves her spot and takes a few steps forward and as many steps back; she presses herself to the walls in the darkness at the end of the alley and counts to four then turns and counts to four again.

Her granddaughter had sat here—right here is where her granddaughter had sat in the light of dawn and nothing out of the ordinary took place; she was dressed in black and drank her breakfast tea as usual, slung the red bag over her shoulder and rushed to work on the corniche as usual.

It was May Day and someone asked *you're not going to the demonstration, are you?* and The Missing One replied *nope* and adjusted her headscarf; she kissed our Pearl, Mo and Minna and said *see ya*, tossed a kiss into the alley and continued the long way on foot to the corniche.

The grandmother remembers that she raised both hands in response and then cursed the arse the girl worked for, saying *I hate that damn corniche and every pig sitting there stuffing themselves by the sea*; the grandmother turned to our Pearl and said *I hate their snouts and suits, their shiny shoes dirtier than mine once you get a good look at them and their well-groomed beards and fat wallets.*

I hope they choke on their own satiety she said as the girl fell out of sight and the girl's mother replied *I know you do, Mum* and continued clearing away the breakfast laid out in the middle of the alley.

The grandchild was her usual self and the same sun rose that day if a little warmer than before and the same milkman came driving by and waved at our Pearl, Mo and Minna where they sat drowsy and happy and waiting for the day to begin; the same bread vendor stopped by with two-day-old bags at half price and the same schoolchildren passed by, turned around, gazed into the alley.

The grandmother remembers how she took out the knitted sweaters the relief organization had left and unravelled them and then sat down to crochet more washcloths and tablecloths to sell outside the grocery stores and on the beach;

she crocheted flowers and lace borders and secured the ends with small beads the children had found in the trash beyond the bookshops and the university.

She got up from time to time to check on the rice, call the children into the shade and sweep away the trash that kept blowing in from the road and clustering in the alley; she washed the children's underpants and asked them to hang them up to dry, then took out slates and writing paper, lifted the odd book from the stacks beside the wall and let the children copy out of and read aloud from it in the alley.

The grandmother closes her eyes, lets out a loud moan.

You couldn't even sit still as a child she says and smooths a hand over her skirt like she used to caress The Missing One, the girl's head in her lap, as she picked up a library book and read in the language she was coming to understand. *Every chance you got you asked to help with the sheet metal walls and the floors and every morning there you were dressed and eager, ready to run and lift and hammer and saw in two. Sometimes when you grew tired of it or were given boring things to do, you would run with a book in hand to the shade by the mountain wall and hide, eating bread and butter if we had any and reheating the morning tea, bringing it to me in a glass, giving me a taste. Every evening right after we'd blown out the candles you would wonder if we would always live by the hillside and the mountain, if you could call it home now, if that could be your wish.*

The grandmother presses her head to the wall, becoming one with it.

I remember your stiff plaits, just below the shoulder, and your favourite red slippers that we managed to take with us at the last minute she says as if into a void—*I remember the first time you got your period and how proud you were the morning you asked me to fasten the hand-me-down bra. I told your mother you needed more time to play and she said, I agree, but it's so hard when she doesn't want to and so it was—you didn't want to play* says the grandmother and keeps crying against the wall—*you had forgotten how, like Naima once forgot, unless you were playing with the children so as, in play, to care for them and protect them, hold them close and teach them.*

The grandmother puts her hand over her eyes, sees nothing and says *no one knew my Naima like I did nor did anyone love her as much, don't you know?*

She moves in darkness through the alley, says *when Naima sat down in front of my hands, I brushed her hair thoroughly and added beads to the plaits across her forehead—white, shining beads that became more like a waterfall the more of her hair I drew in and the longer the hair was on the sides and at the back of her neck.*

The grandmother says *I borrowed her sweater and she my panties sometimes—I took her new headscarf and she my books sometimes. Sometimes she would bring me a piece of red beetroot she had saved and kept cutting the mould off of, pressing it to her lips and cheeks, and sometimes she would stand outside our door and cry, saying she was lonely, that I must stay with her always, anything else would be impossible. The next day she'd usually have calmed down and we'd smoke or play cards, paint our nails with polish she had snuck out of the shop nearest the food storehouse and then we'd read—me out loud and she with her head on my lap.*

In the pit the darkness is almost interminable and nothing gets through to the grandmother except the sound of the grandchildren, who time and time again stumble on the ground in their bare feet and in falling strike their knees where they'd struck them before.

The grandchildren don't cry and if they do start crying they soon stop and if they fall again they don't bother to get up.

Each time the grandmother is about to leave her pit and approach the children, to dust them off and carry them in her arms—pressing a kiss to a forehead or shoulder and letting them cry a while with their faces to her chest—but she soon notices that the children don't want this and so she leaves it be.

From her pit she asks instead *how did it go?* and *does it hurt?* and waits, asking *should I come over?* and *have you hurt yourself?* and keeps on waiting.

For a moment everything is unmoving, as if the street has fallen through space-time into nothingness.

Then the grandmother strains her ears, turns them to the ruined wall and the alley and listens.

Is someone coming down the road and will they then head for the alley?

Are they accompanied by loss, coming to take the children away, or are they coming to stay, to remain here, to make sure that all is returned and goes back to how it used to be in the alley?

3

Friday afternoon, late summer soon autumn in the part of the city where the abandoned houses crowd alongside the renovated and whitewashed ones farther on, and the overgrown alleys hold the mounds of trash bigger and more corrosive between collections ever more infrequent or even not at all.

Do I have three or four children now the woman says quietly to herself as she steps into the alley in full glare and sees the children half-asleep, dusty, and the walls on one side collapsing.

Is there anything left of her to carry with me when I go she says and moves as softly as she can among the bags of thick sweaters and pants no one does anything with anymore *and will it make me more whole if I carry it with me?* as she lifts the broken curtain, their bathroom door, and steps inside.

Her mother sees her from the darkness in the alley denser than before and calls her name, saying *are you back, my darling?* and falls silent in anticipation of any response at all from her daughter; the grandmother looks at the emaciated daughter-body and how she, without lifting hand or gaze, continues into the bathroom and so says nothing more—doesn't say *shall I make us some tea* or *we have bread in a tin somewhere, shall I get it out?* She doesn't call out *have you had any news* or *let me have a look at you before the children take you* when she sees the grandchildren now awake after their slumber following their mother to the curtain and into the bathroom.

The woman searching for her child looks around. The washtub, the water scoop and the stump of soap are in the same corner as always and half-hidden under the sink are also the scissors, the comb and the wooden stool the children sit on when she cuts their hair that big hair and styles it; the same toilet seat cold against the children's bottom is there and the same lampshade cracked and left hanging since the war. The woman looks for something to dry herself with and then approaches the broken bathtub and shelf just above, sees the soap that The Missing One loved wrapped up tight in plastic and newspaper and weighs it gently in her hand.

Before putting it in her bag she brings it to her nose and flinches, then lets it drop into the flyers at the bottom and folds her clothes almost no clothes left into a pile, runs the water. The woman drops another soap with a different scent and colour into the water by turns tepid by turns cold and roughly scrubs the wash-cloth she once crocheted herself over her arms and under her breasts, rinses herself clean; she pours large scoops of water over her bruised body and washes behind her ears and in the bends of her knees, pushing the liquid out of her toenails and peeling the scab off the wound on her thigh.

Mum our Pearl finally ventures in the door-way where she has been standing with her older siblings behind her, watching their mother's naked back in anticipation of her turning around just once—*have you found her yet?*

Our Pearl ventures into the bathroom and is now standing as close to her mother as she can get and asks *are you going to stay with us now?* and *shall we fix you dinner? We have beans and tomato* our Pearl says—*maybe a little oil too if you like and maybe some plums* she says. Our Pearl waits for their mother to reply as the alley quivers, its stones as beautiful in the same light as before and the cats in the same repose under the palms across the road.

The woman recognizes herself as she moves half-dressed past the children and towards the sleeping spot to which she ever more rarely returns, but still sees that neither the alley nor the sleeping spot are what they once were; she recognizes her legs and the scar drawn across her chest and knows that on her neck is a birthmark and from the corner of her mouth a cut, but she still does not understand whose body it is that she's looking at in the mirror shard dusty leaning against one wall in the alley.

If the body is hers, why is it still here?

If it's still here, why is it unfit?

Unable to protect and embrace, she no longer knows what to do with her body other than to lay it in the sand at night and press the cigarette butts she has collected glowing into her arms and legs, falling asleep afterwards; she knows no more than to, at dawn, walk into the sea and wash her wounds clean and then to, again, sleep wet in the wet sand, wait for the sun, wake up ready to go.

All the while the children stand or sit beside her, watching her; all the while, as if she were a gift, the children count the marks on her shoulders and then use their fingers to draw in the dust in the alley; the children forget the stones they usually play with at this time of day and want nothing more than to sit with their mum now that she is back at last, *isn't that right, Mum? Aren't you back now, at least for one night?* our Pearl asks and sinks down again.

The children seek her out those times she returns and then want to be held like they were held before the girl was among the missing—warmed and tickled, cuddled and scolded like before the act of waiting for The Missing One leached everything from the alley—and so lie down next to her where she with her face to the wall no longer bats away the cockroaches and rats, the dust and sheets of newspaper from the road; the children ask her to sing the song they sang when the hillside was still standing and the mountain water flowed in soft cold gulps with which to cool themselves in the morning, and then want to have her close, *here on my bed* our Pearl says and reaches out an arm and *no on my bed* says Minna and pulls her mother to her; the children seek her out, but not as eagerly as before and she can see it—she sees that for fear of her disappearing they are not pushing as hard and not pulling her hair as they once did, not hitting her arms and legs in the hopes of being spoken to or shouted at, nor turning her face towards theirs round smooth, right up close.

No, she sees that the alley has changed and so does not on this Friday push away the children as she has previously done; she does not avoid their gazes and does not keep them out of her arms as resolutely, no longer sits silent awhile after they first call out *Mum* and then her name again and again and does not say *no* or *wait* when they ask for a story and then one more across the alley.

Today the world feels different somehow new and when the woman wakes up after a nap, the afternoon sun low and the children sleeping beside, she turns her whole body to the children and draws them near.

What mother doesn't take her own life after a child disappears?

The woman sits the children in front of her and smooths their hair stroke upon stroke from forehead to nape.

Well, yes, she does recognize herself—ever since May Day she has again and again rejected the children for fear of softening and in that softness forgetting that she must always be searching, has worn the same expression and the same smile as before, but neither she nor the children are the same.

Before she goes, she leaves all but three flyers and gives the children a firm kiss on the cheek.

She knows how to get from the alley to the road, from the library to the square, and then to the corniche—that is where she is going, it's towards the restaurant and the corniche that she is moving.

Friday afternoon one late summer in a city where schoolchildren on their way home among the cars stop at newspaper stands and buy lollipops buy ice cream, stand next to the magazines and flip through comics that they aren't allowed to bring home.

The schoolchildren don't mind the passersby in the afternoon rushing past, whacking them every now and then with a tote or grocery bag, foot or stroller; they don't look up, don't move on until they've finished reading their comic and the afternoon traffic has begun to thin out across the city.

In the alley our Pearl, Minna and Mo sit next to the stone labyrinths and think about their mother who has just disappeared around the corner beyond the ruined wall towards the square and the library.

The children know that the greengrocer is at his busiest at this time of day when many customers are asking for carrots asking for cucumbers and understand that this is why their mother is in a rush; hoping to pass by unnoticed and avoid having to hear the greengrocer ask about The Missing One and the children she left in the alley, their mother crosses the square, her strides as long as she can make them, and continues to the small door at one end.

The children can see her—in their inner eye they can see her limping, her headscarf slightly crooked—and want to shout something to their mother, perhaps something loud and unkind, but perhaps something else, tender and healing.

Today their mother feels different somehow new and the children lie down in the middle of the alley and reach out a hand for the smoothest stone, put it to their mouth. They think of how they'd just been resting in her arms and been kissed on the cheek and tummy, and they close their eyes as they lie beside the mountain in the middle of the alley, leaving the stone on their lips.

Afternoon, the slowness interminable in the alley.

The children no longer move beyond this ruined wall and the depth and width of the alley, no longer walk down the street except for matches and palm fronds, a little tea and a little sugar and maybe a little almond oil with which to wash their hair the times their grandmother steps out of the darkness and shouts *the water's warm* and the children hurry to scoop and pour, scrub and rinse.

The children don't go to the sea anymore either—not to play or to work with the other children there, not to swim or sit there, not to pick shells or collect stones or build sandcastles and waterways that flow to the reeds; the children do not wash their wounds in the salt water or look for jewellery in the sand dunes, do not search for their sister like they searched for her in the early days and, refusing to sit still or keep quiet, do not burn any more tires or plastic chairs in piles on the road.

Yes, in the early days the children refused to wait for their mother to return from her increasingly endless searches in the city, nor did they want to listen to their grandmother who crying asked them to stay put, to stay home and not leave her on her own in the alley.

No, the children wanted to move onward and forward, and only until the night they were driven to the police station did they stop searching for their sister in the city.

The grandmother picked them up and held them close in sleep almost no sleep at all and then muttered that no one beyond the ruined wall wished them well and that she couldn't bear another loss—again and again she said she couldn't bear any more loss and even though the children didn't understand how or why, they knew the loss was now a part of them and at any moment it could strike again.

The children continue to take stones lost from the ruined wall and place them on their mountain, turning it into a home, raising it as a shelter.

Remember the glass jar Mum took to the beach and filled with sand and seawater and carried all the way back home? the children ask each other and look to where they last saw their grandmother sitting or speaking into the alley.

Yes, Mum loves the sea even though she's not much of a swimmer and doesn't dare go out too far the children reply and search along the walls and rubble for a cockroach or an ant, a centipede, a spider or a rat running up and lingering in the alley.

Remember that night when she came home from work at the corniche with wounds all over her back and Mum and Gran told her she had to stop working at that bloody corniche? the children ask each other and stick a finger through the new hole in their sweater, still the best one they have.

Yes, I remember the children say—*they taught her to crochet washcloths but she never did take to it and then she said it wasn't about that—there was more to it than her not working on the corniche anymore, it wasn't just about her quitting her job there* they say and take off their favourite sweater, wash it in the cracked sink still damp from their mother and put it back on wet.

No, right the children say—*she said they'd only keep beating and thieving and closing the locks and there has to be a stop to what goes on at the corniche* the children say and lie down, warming themselves in the sun, sleeping again.

If we pray to God as many times as there are stones in the mountain we built, maybe one day she'll come back the children say to each other and look out at the labyrinths still in pretty circles across the alley.

If we jump on one leg and spell out her name with each jump and each rhyme, maybe Mum will find her and they'll come home as soon as tonight the children say and again move towards the mountain, the only thing waiting for them in the alley.

Later, just as darkness begins to fall and they move across the road towards the palm groves for leaves and twigs to burn before sleep, the children find a soft ball under one of the piles and bring it back with them.

Mo holds the ball as tightly as he can, not daring to hand it over, not bouncing or rolling it in his hands until they have crossed the road and are once again standing behind the ruined wall in the alley; he does not help his siblings as they collect the labyrinth stones for the mountain now larger than ever, and no longer hears the car horns and juice vendors moving and shouting on the road leading to the city and the corniche.

Then Mo finally throws the ball to our Pearl and Minna and watches them kick it between them for a while—first calmly and slowly and then more and more eagerly until they run right out of energy.

If you throw it in the air, I'll catch it after one bounce Minna says and waits in the twilight now smooth and red across the alley—*if you catch it after one bounce, I'll catch it after two* our Pearl says and takes up position, waiting for Mo to throw the ball again and for the game to begin here in the alley.

4

Friday evening one late summer or autumn in a seaside town with a beach and a university, its small courtyard open to a square with corn vendors and juice stands and booksellers and a library.

The woman who is searching for her child recognizes the grocery stores she sometimes sat outside with necklaces and crocheted washcloths neatly arranged on a skirt, and remembers at what time the restaurants set out their evening menus and the cafés pack in their patios; she recognizes the cleaners who move through the same places at the same times every day, and knows where the health centre is where she took The Missing One and without presenting any documents turned the girl around and pulled up her sweater. The girl had wounds from working on the corniche and when the nurse saw her, she took her in and washed the wounds clean, dressed them and administered painkillers to help the girl sleep.

The woman remembers that behind the hotel in the farthest corner, where everyone ignores her now, two palms grow paler with each passing day and farther along at the bend next to the bus stop sits a tobacconist with whom she usually talks on the days when it's possible to talk at all. *Have you found her yet?* he asks each time he sees the woman coming and when she doesn't answer he hands her a cigarette and if she can manage to say *not yet* he hands her two.

Will I get to see her when I die or right before death? the woman asks out loud now on the square near the library and the fountain and *is what my grandmother said true—that you meet the children you've lost as if on a path and they follow you in?* she says and passes the park benches and the cherry trees, the shop windows and the playground.

If we meet in a dream she says and continues past the schoolchildren lollipops in hand leaning over the flowing fountain—*if she calls my name once more as in a question or game and asks me to come* she says and sees the office buildings on the left and the tailor's shop on the corner, the restaurant she once promised to take the children to and the greengrocer who despite the rush at the cart notices her limping along and runs to meet her on the square.

The greengrocer wants to talk to her and to embrace her, asks if she would like to sit down and rest awhile, then tells her he already visited the children this morning and dropped off some bread and some fruit, *some beans and some vegetables* he says *and I told them to make sure to drink plenty. I have told the children not to go out on the road except for palm fronds and tea* he says *and warned them not to go with the men I've heard visit the alley claiming to know where the girl is or where you are sleeping at night—have you heard about that?*

The greengrocer seeks her gaze, is either walking behind or beside her and finally stops, takes her hand.

Have you heard? he repeats, facing the cart and everyone he has left in the line—*have you heard about the men who make their way to the alley at night and try to lure the children away?*

Later that same evening by the railing on the corniche, the woman remembers The Missing One as if she were closer now and as beautiful and regal as ever; the woman sees the girl walking not along a hard slick corniche, but on a sandy beach with sun chairs and a parasol, towels laid out in rows at the water and the air warm, one spring or early summer in the city.

The Missing One walks the outskirts of the shoreline with her younger siblings following behind and carefully searches the sand; the children wait for her to call *come* or *hurry* and then with their pants up high they run to her pointing hand and fall into reverent silence.

Look how lovely this one is The Missing One says and holds up a shell or stone to the sun. *Do you think it fell from the cliffs?* she says—*or is it a gift from the god of the sea or the stars?* The girl says *have you ever seen anything so lovely?* while the younger siblings shake their head and then *here you go* before she hands the stone to our Pearl, now overjoyed on the shoreline.

Does the woman remember this?

Yes, she remembers that day The Missing One said *it might be all right here* and continuing along the beach where the sun chairs were fewer and no white tourists sat up and peered over their sunglasses, watching them surreptitiously or openly the closer they came; the girl went to where the lifeguards would not ask her to get out of the water and shouted from there *it might actually be all right here, Mum—can you imagine?* before she stripped down to her underwear and ran into the water.

The greengrocer asks if there is anything at all he can do and the woman replies *no* and *thank you*, replies *fine* and *I don't know* and then hurries on across the square.

At the library those working the counter that day ask how she's doing and tell her that no one has called, not yet at least, but maybe soon, says the new librarian, who then asks if the woman might like to make more copies of the flyer or add a phone number to the image.

Perhaps you'd like to tell me more about how she was dressed and if she walks or stands in a particular way? Do you have the names of her friends and over the years did she acquire a scar or mark that isn't visible in the photo that you might be able to tell us about?

The woman shakes her head and says *no* and *I don't know*, says *no, I don't think so* as best she can and then *there is no more recent picture—they took everything* as if she needed to catch her breath between each word.

She speaks almost inaudibly and feels then, as she does several times a day, out of sorts; when her eyes fall on the poster with the photo of The Missing One dressed in her best pants and sweater by the ditch between the former homes on the hillside, she once again knows where in life she is and walks to the door.

The woman says *thank you* and *I have to go now* to those who have brought tea and cake and then *you are very kind but I really must go* before she continues out of the room.

The people working the counter that day follow her and promise that the phone is in working order and the answering machine is on; they say that the long-awaited call will one day come, they can feel it, and just as the woman hears this, she steps out into the twilight and crosses the road.

Twilight soon night above a city where the students always the last to leave the library have gathered around the dented car door, carried here from the junkyard to light a fire of palm fronds and twigs atop, bake bread and fry thinly sliced potatoes and set a teapot on the flat stones beside.

The students sit with their backs to the stark new building, mix the batter of flour, salt and water, and share between them what vegetables and fruit they have; they remove their socks and shoes, then take out their books, quizzing each other to prepare for the final seminar tomorrow, reading aloud and demonstrating.

The children in the alley haven't started to freeze even though at this time of day they usually sit around the fire not too big so the wind won't carry it off.

Yes, at this time of day the children in the alley usually lie down in the dark next to what used to be a wall and is now mostly rubble, and cover themselves with the blanket, look up at the sky—do they see anything there? The children usually straighten their pillows, no more than two sweaters around which their grandmother sewed a piece of sheet, and press their feet together, hold their hands like binoculars and then continue to search the sky—do they see a star or moon or the light sailing from the moon down towards their faces now cast blue in the alley? Do they see Venus, *the brightest of stars* as The Missing One used to say, and with Venus in sight, can they orient themselves further across the sky?

But not tonight.

Tonight the world feels different somehow new and the ball the children are still kicking between them feels harder and newer with each thud against the ruined wall—shinier each time our Pearl picks the ball up with her hands even though that's not allowed and more beautiful, yes it's almost sheer beauty, each time Minna manages a header or chest trap.

The children say *kick it to me* and take a leap across the alley, say *here* and stand wide-legged, at the ready.

The children play long after the streetlamp shines red on the mountain of stones piled in the middle of the alley and it is not until the ball, kicked from one side to the other, ricochets somehow and rolls off to the pit at one end of the alley that the children stop playing.

The children stand there, watching the ball go.

They wait for it to bounce back or for Gran to toss it their way, but nothing happens and no ball is returned to the game and the children in the alley.

It's not actually a pit Mo says and looks at the dark beneath Gran's tarp, in the daytime the only shade in the alley—*after all it's just the darkness from where Gran watches over us* he says and waits, grabbing his head.

When neither ball nor grandmother appears, the children eventually move into the darkness to search for the ball there.

From time to time they look back at the road and the mountain glowing red, and then go farther in.

The children move first to where the light from the streetlamp seeps in and a sparse darkness envelops and enfolds; here they see their ragged sweaters in a pile and plastic bags folded neatly beneath a rock, the books no one reads anymore in stacks by the wall and farther away a notebook The Missing One would write in from time to time.

The children lift the pad out of the dust and cold and tuck it under their sweater, carry it with them.

Then they go deeper in and soon the darkness is heavier and harder for them to navigate—soon they can no longer discern anything but shadows and contours and soon the cold makes its way in and turns their young bodies stiff.

Is this the same alley where they've been sleeping and eating and fighting and playing, with the same depth and the same shade, the same bullet holes in the walls and the same bed where Gran used to sit or lie and from there look out across the alley?

Was it this deep before too, and this dark and cold and impossible?

The children don't know yet keep going, catching sight of a rope and their old slingshot still intact and take the slingshot with them—see a pair of scissors Gran forgot to put away and Mum's soft shawl and pocket them both; the children see the vague outline of the slate no one uses anymore and the camping stove they gathered around in the evenings now overturned and finally also a teapot, a sugar bowl and a comb broken in two.

The children carry everything back out into the alley then return to the darkness, move farther in.

The ball is nowhere to be seen.

Do you remember the cats in the afternoons? the children ask each other as they search the depths of the alley.

I remember their golden fur, one soft the other coarse, and the scratch of their tongues against my hand the children reply, now almost completely invisible in the alley.

Do you remember the ditch and the water rippling in the ditch? the children ask each other, crouching in the darkness by the wall.

I remember my feet in that rippling water and your laughter the children say to each other and drag their hand through the dust, trying to find what has disappeared and is no longer present in the alley.

The children drag a cold hand from one side to the other, once and then once more.

They do this many times and eventually come to a standstill in the dark. Then Minna says *it's ours, you have to give it back* and waits awhile; she says *if you don't want to give it back to us, we'll come get it when it's light out and the sun is at its highest point and the mirror will help us find our way to you* and then she awaits no answer out in the alley.

Before the children make their way back, they find The Missing One's old jewellery box and take that too, wiping it with their sweater, carrying it under their arm.

Do you remember the tins we filled with mud? the children ask each other as they slowly move towards the mountain, gathering the palm fronds and twigs into a pile and lighting the fire.

I remember the tin cans and how to fill them without getting cut the children reply as they pour beans on bread atop a sheet of newspaper and settle down in the alley.

Do you remember how the sun would sink over the hillside and make night of the mist clouding above our homes? the children ask each other and take out their mother's shawl from their pocket, hold it up to the streetlight and the black sky, then spread it out in the alley.

I remember the sun, the mist and our homes the children say to each other and place The Missing One's notebook, jewellery box, and everything else they have taken on the shawl now hidden behind the mountain in the alley.

Later the children will make room for a kitchen with a hotplate and two pots and a corner for the clothes and the jewellery box; they will put the laundry tub in a corner and hang a rope along the wall for the clothes to dry in the sun, and perhaps take out the slate and sometimes a book as well, settling down in the alley.

Friday night and a darkness deeper than before descends, advances on the children brilliant red in the streetlight's shine and touches them in play and laughter with the ball they have found and are now kicking around the alley.

The moment the grandmother sees the children carrying in the ball she stands up, keeps an eye on it and keeps an eye on the children's game in the alley. Sometimes when the big stone mountain the children have built obscures them and causes them to vanish from sight for a moment, she prepares to dash out, screaming their names. And sometimes when the ball rolls towards the ruined wall and the pavement and keeps going as if headed straight for the traffic on the road, she turns away, refusing to watch the children follow after it, refusing to watch them die out on the road.

The grandmother feels for the first time in a long time an autumn chill and wonders if she should light the fire herself—does she remember how? She takes one step forward but doesn't come any closer to the children and then wonders where the matches are and the lighter fluid, have they been used up? She wonders if the children have gone off to procure such things or if she should do it herself and then sits down, *no, how?* the grandmother says out loud in the depths of the alley—*it's not possible* she says and falls back against the wall.

Had you been here now, you'd be calling for them to eat and saying it's already late and the fire must be lit and the ball put away the grandmother says and points to a spot on the ground in front of her as if The Missing One were there. *You would have told them to get some sleep even if there are no more school days and that the relief organization might show up tomorrow and give them new notebooks and new pencils, new coloured drawing paper and a new writing board, who knows?* the grandmother says and tries to keep warm by softly dancing around the end of the alley.

We were inseparable, my Naima and I, have I told you about that? she says as if whispering to The Missing One. *Perhaps not as inseparable as you and I, of course—if you wanted to go to the sugarcane fields, I'd come along and if you wanted more books to read, we'd walk to the library together* the grandmother says—*still Naima and I were inseparable.*

The morning her little brother knocked on the door and told me she had disappeared, I'd just sat down to eat some bread and cheese. He asked if I knew where she was and I remember thinking he looked sloppy in his unironed shirt and muddy slippers, hair uncombed and no bag or belt. I said no and told him we'd last seen each other the previous night when we'd sat by the fountain drinking sodas and smoking a cigarette. I said that she'd told me about her job and that she was tired of riding the bus and that she'd prefer to work somewhere else nearby the grandmother says and keeps moving through the alley, watching the children's game and intermittently closing her eyes as if she were wishing for the impossible.

Later when more and more girls disappeared and the boys were in the war or in prison, not one person kept looking for my Naima or the green sweater and cotton pants I knew she was wearing that night. I'd told them—I described what she was wearing and said I knew she had my pink panties because she'd borrowed them that day—but the police said they'd found nothing and had nothing to go on.

The grandmother dances, wishing for the impossible, and when the ball slowly rolls into her part of the alley, she picks it up and doesn't give it back.

As she continues to watch the children as they approach the depths of the alley in search of the ball—creeping through the darkness and carrying out everything she has been storing in her part of the alley since the girl became one of the missing—she moves in deeper, to a place she did not know the alley contained, and is soon no longer seen in the alley.

If you'd been here the grandmother says *we'd have stayed up while the others were sleeping and smoked the butts I saved, drunk our tea. We'd have lit the kerosene lamp again and I'd have put my head in your lap—you'd have read to me and then we'd have talked about what it was going to be like when you finally stopped working on that bloody corniche* the grandmother says, clutching the ball in her hands more tightly.

5

Night one Friday soon autumn in a city where the noise from the corniche wakes the street dogs who, shielded by the reeds and the stacked sun chairs, are dozing at one end of the beach; each time the tourists hoot, they wake up and bark—each time the music gets louder and the wind finds its way to where they're curled up with their muzzles pressed into the sand, they lift their heads and fall back asleep, and so it continues the whole night through to dawn, until there is no one still drinking and eating on the corniche.

The woman searching for her child approaches the restaurant where The Missing One once worked and sits down on a bench opposite, looks around. A few restaurants away you also happen to be sitting, talking to your co-workers about the architecture and the food in the city.

They haven't quite got tipsy yet and started girl-watching and you have yet to take your walk, to look for another spot along the corniche.

The woman is no longer wearing a headscarf or slippers and doesn't have it in her to shout *hello* or *come here* when she sees a girl heading to the kitchen across the restaurant floor; she offers no reply when a man addresses her from the road and does not look over at the grill kiosks or the harbour.

Of all my children, she is the one I miss the most the woman says out loud and remembers the girl walking here one night with a sack or bag in her hand—*of all the people I talk to in my mind, she is the one I want to hear* she says and remembers that it was to or from the market that they were going and that they had just sat down to rest when the girl stood right back up and started walking towards the alley.

The woman remembers that the girl's hair was still long in plaits down her back and that she hadn't yet been bruised on her arms and legs; she remembers that they had talked about her younger siblings and why they hadn't been allowed to start school and that the light had been both dawning and gloaming, whichever it was, it was a light to which she wanted to return.

Yes, the light may have been of the dawn streaked pink or green, or of the dusk like the light was before the girl disappeared when the sun would sink towards the mountains and the harbour and the city would take on a soft almost hazy darkness, inviting and warm, a light less violent than the light now.

No, the light was different and brittle back then, not blinding like now, and she saw that the girl was lost in thought and for once did not ask what or who or how or why; the woman just walked beside her daughter and said nothing the whole way except once as the alley drew near and the girl put the sack down and crossed the road to enter the palm groves on the other side.

At that moment—just as the girl reappeared holding palm fronds as big as she was—the woman said *I wish you wouldn't take that job on the corniche* and then fell silent, taking the fronds from the girl's arms and listening to her say that she'd already made up her mind and it was going to be fine—that she was not alone in working there and together they were strong, it would work out one way or another, she knew it would.

The woman takes her bag off, sets it on the bench where she is sitting across from the restaurant, now with patrons at every table on the patio. Tonight the music is unbearable, pulsing hard throughout the corniche, still every now and then she can hear the tourists howling with laughter or asking for more to drink, can see them as they stop to look at her and then continue as idly as before across the corniche.

When the children who are following the food approach her and ask if she would like some chicken or some of the bread they've managed to rustle up on the corniche, she has the energy to take them in her arms and tell them she has eaten and is very full; when they ask *are you sure?* the woman says she has never eaten as much and then *now you must eat just as much—you understand that, right?*

Is your sister feeling better? she asks the girl holding her younger sibling's hand and then *I know a good health centre where she can go. Have you all found a place to sleep?* she asks the boy beside her and then *I know a place where you can go.*

After the woman has described the way to the alley and told the children that in the alley they will find both a place to sleep and friends, she opens her bag and takes out the girl's soap, puts it to her nose. Then she takes the knife out of her pocket and holds it in her hand and finally one of the photos of The Missing One, which she kisses before turning to face the tourists and the restaurant on the corniche.

I am searching for my daughter the woman will then say as loudly and clearly as she can.

She worked here on the corniche and it is for her sake that I have come she will say while standing outside the entrance to the restaurant.

Saturday morning a different perhaps milder light upon the city.

Do you remember what she was like at the library? the children say to each other when they at dawn rise from their beds and peer into the darkness, checking to see if the ball has resurfaced or if Gran has tossed it into the alley. *Do you remember which book was her favourite, the one she always used to read sitting against the armchair on the rug even if the armchair was free and she could just as well have sat in it?* the children ask and wash their face and neck, run a hand through their hair.

Do you remember we once asked her why she didn't sit in the armchair when it was free and she shook her head and said she couldn't bear anyone looking at her as if she were soiling it? Do you remember that she then picked us up and put us in the armchair instead and said that we should never think that of ourselves, that we were soiling things? the children ask each other as they watch the sun rise over the rooftops across the street and listen to the traffic get heavier and maybe somewhere a chirping bird, a barking dog.

The children nod and say *I don't know what the book is called, but I remember what it looked like and what it was about—maybe the librarians will know what it's called if we tell them she was reading it?* and then take out bread and beans, fruit and oil in the alley.

Yes, I'm sure they'll know what it's called, but I don't dare go in case she or Mum come home and I'm not here the children say, mouth full of breakfast.

I dare, but I don't want to go either in case she or Mum comes home and none of us are here the children reply and lie down, waiting for the sun to rise high and for them to make their way to where Gran is and find the ball, toss it back out.

It is then or soon thereafter that the children from the corniche walk into the alley and see a mountain of stones rise up and obscure the view of the children and the grandmother they have heard about and who are said to live in the alley; later, they are not sure exactly when, but it is then or soon after that the children in the alley hear a *hello?* and pick up a stone and stand at the ready, guarding everything laid out on the shawl in the alley.

Later the children from the corniche explain how they ended up there and ask if what the woman had said last night is true—that they can sleep and eat here, rest and warm themselves a while?

Is it true your sister has disappeared and she had short hair that only went down to here? the children from the corniche say and our Pearl, Mo and Minna nod, saying *she worked on the corniche, we don't know where she is* before they take out tins of beans to dish out and set water out in the sun for the children to wash themselves with later.

Our Pearl, Mo and Minna show the children from the corniche the fallen walls facing the construction sites and the bathroom with the ceiling torn down as well as the sweater they can put on if they feel cold.

Finally they show them the spot where the grandmother can no longer be seen and say *our ball is back there—let's go get it and then perhaps we can play together here in the alley.*

THE SINGULARITY

Early winter, soon snowfall across a city where the buses to the centre roll in and lower down for the mothers who coffee in hand manoeuvre the strollers and take a seat.

Later you remember that the autumn was unusually mild and the blanket your sister gave you lay smoothed on the cot next to the wall, awaiting the child. You remember that earlier in the night you had chopped parsley for Gran's eggplant stew recipe and that the picture of the cactus flower you had put up with a few pieces of tape had fallen to the floor, that you couldn't find it when, belly in the way, you were looking under the bed. The hill outside the kitchen window had by lunchtime already gone as dark as a mountain or the closest thing to a mountain you have come across since childhood, and you had started to think of the dream you'd had the night before in which the baby was finally born, was already six months old and had big black hair like Rozia.

Later you also remember how your mother set aside her tea glass to help you on with your winter boots and jacket, held you tightly as you shopped for the baby's first clothes and a purple plush rabbit.

Take especial care in this mild winter she said, leaning against the galleria with its bread and cheese stalls outside—*before you know it, you'll have taken a fall* she said *and we can do without that sort of accident* as she bent over to read the price per kilo of string cheese and white cheese and lost her footing and slipped.

You remember that earlier in the day she had commented on the photo of the girl that, ever since you found it in the woman's bag on the corniche, you'd been saving in your notebook open on the kitchen table. She had said *so lovely* and *so pretty*, asked you if you saved the soap, and then *I understand.*

Later you remember how in the weeks before you went on long walks in hopes of inducing labour and how every day you bought the sweet bread you liked and took it to the hill that soothed and rocked you, talked you through it. You bought two big bags of detergent and hard soap and carried them up the stairs, unpacked for want of anything else to do the little bag of tiny pyjamas and socks and once more washed everything by hand.

That morning your brother called to say he had bought a onesie with teddy bear ears on the hood and a little later your sister got in touch asking about washcloths, if you had enough or if she should pick some up now while she was out shopping. *You need at least eight or ten* she said as you nodded down at the phone and pulled out each one of your towels, wondering which of them to cut up and re-sew.

You shouldn't worry so much, your co-worker said between bites of lunch in the cafeteria bathed in winter light—do you remember this?

You shouldn't always imagine the worst and should understand that the child is calmer towards the end as there is less space, she said, and helped herself to yet another piece of potato, wiped her mouth. You were talking about the trip and about the corniche, and she asked you if you'd finished writing the report and you said *no, not yet—I haven't been able to get my thoughts in order* you say and put down your cutlery—*I keep coming back to the woman on the corniche and then it's impossible for me to write, do you know what I mean?* you say and take a sip of water.

Later first and foremost you will remember the light in the examination room and how you listened to the doctor tell you what you needed to do and that you could go home for the night if you wanted to, hearing her say how many people preferred that, to be in a safe place so to speak.

Your first *no* shocked them, made them back off. Later when they tried to take your hand, you slapped them away and when they asked if it was home you were going to, you replied *I have no home* and kept walking.

You stay in that room for a very long time.

For years you wander the windowless corridor, it's like a canal lock between the reception and the maternity ward, and when someone asks you to tell them what it was like, you tell them what you remember, but each time using new words and in a different order.

You say *I remember there was a family sitting in the waiting room and I greeted them. It was dark and the grandmother was the only one who returned my greeting. She had a bag in her arms, it was green, and later I also saw the child slumped in the chair next to her, kicking the rug away again and again.*

You say *I remember drinking two glasses of cold water that night and knowing afterwards that it was over, do you know what I mean? That's how the story always goes, I know, but I was certain that neither the sleep nor the tea nor the books nor even the hill could calm me down and that it was once again time for me to go.*

You say *it was the same scene playing itself out, but in a different time and for a moment it occurred to me that supper ought to be cleared away so as not to attract the neighbour's cat, can you imagine? In that moment I thought about how we used to say that it was the neighbour's cat who'd trick the rooster into coming over and it was the rooster who'd sent the dishes crashing to the floor and Mum would get angry, but not at the cat.*

I thought about how from here on out I wouldn't be able to play with the cat anymore and how sad Rozia would be if we didn't get to carry it across the mud pits to the other side of the road and into our playhouse with the red rag rug and the pillows, the hand puppet that belonged to Rozia and the colouring book that belonged to me. Then I walked to the door, took my jacket and wallet and turned both locks.

All I wanted was for the bus to leave on time you say and look out the window.

It was all I could think about, and although it almost never runs as it should, it did then, can you imagine? You almost laugh, can't help it. *That night public transport didn't let me down* you say and sink back into the hospital bed, falling asleep and sleeping long.

When did the child die? you ask the nurses after they've moved you to another room and check on you from time to time, roll up the sleeve of your white shirt, take your blood pressure.

When do you think my baby died? you ask one more time as the nurse notes something down on her pad and before she has a chance to say that unfortunately she will only be able to know after the baby has been born and examined, you turn away and say *well, anyway I think I know—I think it died a long time ago or on the corniche. Maybe it died long before I got here and maybe even before they dug Rozia out, who knows.*

You sit up, adjust the sheet and blanket, try to sound your smoothest.

I mean, maybe the child had already died before I was born and Mum was just a girl, or maybe even before Mum was born and Gran was carrying her and me, do you know what I mean? You clear your throat, try to get some air. *Back when Gran had already lost two children and for fear of losing the third stopped working the vegetable fields and took up sewing—maybe that's when my child died?* you say, looking back at the nurse. *When the train rolled in, and we jumped off and Mum was searching the station and I asked where we were going and she said, wait a minute—just wait here, and stared right at the tracks* you say and fall silent.

Before she leaves you say yes to tea and a sandwich, say you'd like to have more fruit cordial, and half an orange if there's one going, followed by a sleeping pill.

Evening, a maternity ward

It's early winter, you're lying on a hospital bed / it's late summer, you're standing with your feet in the sea—can you see it happening?

Sitting in the waiting room outside, from here on out there is always a grandmother with a bag in her arms and a child slumped in the chair next to her / in the air a fresh chill but the water as mild as before and the corniche as bright and ornate / the nurse rubs her hand over your belly, making it sticky / you're wearing a black dress that gets tighter when you sit when you walk / then looks at you apologetically / the sun hat on your head frames your face and falls forward each time you look down at your belly when you feel the baby kicking, delighted by the sunlight and the heat / sometimes it's hard to tell the mother's heartbeat from the baby's, she says, and rolls a shopping cart over / the passenger plane roaring low over the bustling city and the mountains a shadow beside / the ultrasound machine works better, the nurse says, and switches the screen on / the palm trees swaying, and beyond them is the juice vendor you stop to chat with each day / the light dim almost dark and soon you begin to feel cold / the only public beach that's empty at this time of day, leaving you and a few street dogs to bathe alone / the nurse keeps searching, this time more gently / and the corniche runs like a wall overhead / finally you ask if something is the matter / it happened that night on the corniche / I'm going to get the doctor, she says, I'll be right back, and then walks out into the brightness of the corridor / when you catch sight of the woman she has already climbed out onto the cliffs, is leaning forward / the first doctor takes the time to greet you, tells you her first and last name, seems kind / the woman's eyes search the corniche / the second doctor says nothing at first / first she looks this way and then that / I'm afraid we can't find a heartbeat, she then says / the cold is different tonight but the darkness the same as before—you feel it as you watch the woman on the corniche / later you remember firmly pulling your hair—that it is the first thing you do / does she see you where you're standing, yet another tourist by the railing? / after that you notice the bed barely contains you, why is that? / no, she probably doesn't see you, blinded by the light from the corniche / your jacket is still hanging on the hook, unchanged / the woman is holding the railing, but what is she planning to do? / to think you chose that jacket tonight—to think you chose the red duffel coat over the black one you otherwise always wear / when she throws herself off maybe you scream *no* across the corniche / why did you do that? / you scream or do not scream *no* across the corniche / in the room only the doctors and the back of the screen to fix your eyes on / the scream is loud, it comes from all directions, but was it you who screamed? / one of the doctors pulls up a chair, starts telling you about the induction of labour, about what's to come / you don't know, you can't remember, have no one to ask / the doctor talks at length, barely looking at you all the while / was something said in the scream or was it just a scream unfurling, do you remember? / you sit up on the bed, clamp a hand over your mouth, look around / it may or may not have been your *no* across the corniche / outside a beeping machine gets louder and louder and now the doctor is finally looking at you / maybe or maybe not your voice across the cliffs, the railing and the racket of traffic along that corniche / then you say *I can't* and try to get away / a stillness as the woman's body disappears, onto the rocks and into the sea / *I won't do it* you say and grab your bag and jacket off the hook / and then the way the corniche just goes back to being as noisy and as bright as before.

No you say as loudly as you can.

The doctors don't understand.

No, I will not birth my baby you say as clearly as you can and then leave the room.

Day 1

Someone has locked the windows facing the hospital courtyard and you can no longer air the room out, you feel breathless / a mattress is put to one side in anticipation of the night, of the baby and mother curling up at night / later the nurse says it's routine and nothing out of the ordinary, that you shouldn't worry about the window / the kerosene lamp casts a yellow light on the ceiling, and along the walls black with soot, a mist spills across the floor / you ask no more questions and turn away, your belly heavy on the bed / in one corner a girl is helping her mother with the day's tasks—do you see them sitting there? / yet another doctor kneels down, takes your hand, says your name twice / it's your mother and her mother, they're busy, trying to finish up / the doctor begs you to understand, says please and lingers / Gran shows the girl how to beat the cotton fluffy and how to finish sewing the quilt that she later ties a silk ribbon around and takes to the wedding on the other side of town / it's not reasonable to carry a child who is no longer alive, the doctor tells you / she pours water from the big clay vessel and washes her face and under her arms, does the same to the giggling girl who soon thereafter runs to fetch a sheet to wrap herself in / it won't bring your child back to life / she dresses the girl in the one pretty dress she owns and plaits what's left of the silk ribbon into her hair / there is no benefit to carrying the child, dead, inside you / before she snuffs out the lamp she's placed in the same corner as God's holy word and a gem-encrusted box that holds a lock of hair from each of her two dead children, she takes the girl aside and says *we're setting off on an adventure* / in the end your body will protest / with the quilt in hand, they walk past the cars on the main road and take the bus to where the girl has never been before / it will reject the child / as they get off, the aviary and the fountain are backlit, the palm trees more lush than anywhere else / you could get a serious infection / wide streets wide houses and large pavements lined with flower beds and carved gates / it could hurt your chances of carrying other children / sometimes the girl hears birds chirping and sometimes a barking dog / you can take this pill, the doctor says / the girl stops, shakes her head—*why are the houses so big, Mum, how many people actually live here?* / it will get the contractions going / Gran keeps going, rings the bell on the gate of the third house, waits / after that we'll follow your cues / *the woman who opened the door was white and radiantly dressed* Mum later tells you / you shouldn't worry at all about the birth, it will go well / *it was the first time I visited a client with your grandmother, and later in the evening I was given pocket money for my trouble* / you will get all the painkillers you need / I didn't know you had children, says the woman as she hands the envelope to Gran and asks the housekeeper to take the quilt into where the music and cheering is rising above the walls and the courtyard / tonight you'll get a sleeping pill and tomorrow we'll get through this together / Gran takes the money, puts it in her bag, shuts it / you just have to take this pill first / *she's my third* says Gran, stroking the now tired and hungry girl's hair / do you think you can take it now? the doctor asks / *and she is my home and my joy* says Gran and carries the girl to the bus / or should I leave it right here? she asks / *afterwards we ate at the grill kiosk closest to our street* / can you hear me? / *when I asked for a soft drink, I got it and when I asked for bread, there was more* / hello there, can you hear me? / *once home, I also got to stay up with the kerosene lamp lit and read for a long time even though it was already late and Mum had fallen asleep on the mattress next to me.*

Later you ask the doctor *what mother doesn't take her own life when a child dies?*

My grandmother lost two children you say and pat your belly. *Has your grandmother lost any children?* you ask before she leaves.

Day 2

I come from a tradition of loss you say to the counsellor the first time he takes his seat opposite you, notebook on his lap, white coat a little too big in the shoulders / green streaks across a spring sky, a mother bleeds for a child she hadn't wanted to keep / *and I don't intend to continue in that tradition* you say and drink your tea / she carried two gas cylinders up the stairs and had an older cousin punch her stomach *but you'd made up your mind* Mum tells you—*you were going to stick around* / the counsellor's name is Alexander or John and in the dream you approach him with a sharp knife in your hand / Mum is losing blood and isn't allowed to put you to her breast even if she wants to / you rest the teacup on your belly like you did when the child was alive and say *from here on out, no one I love will be forced to give up their child—that ends now, that trauma* / later, when she is given you to hold, she sees that you're the baby from that dream she once had, that it was all real / to birth your child—is that continuing a tradition of loss? Michael or

Anders asks and picks up his pen as if about to make note of something / *That's when I understood the deeper meaning of your arrival* Mum says and kisses your shoulder, the highest point she can reach / outside the first snow, a gloaming light and the occasional ambulance / *what meaning?* you ask later as the two of you stroll the hospital grounds / sometimes there are sounds from the corridor, birthing pains and the cries of infants and midwives saying things you can't comprehend / Mum answers *the meaning of this moment—that you and I are talking like this* and holds you tight so as not to slip in the snow / *I had a friend called Rozia* you say as if speaking to no one / *after the birth I was so broken that we stayed in hospital for a week* she says and wipes her nose / *we were neighbours, Rozia and I, best friends too / and when we finally left, it was already summer, can you imagine? / we were the same age, but she was shorter and fairer, freckled all over / water was flowing in the fountain again and the cherries were in bloom / when her house was bombed no one said a thing to me for years / I had money for a taxi so we took one, you and I / then they told me about how they'd recognized her dress / in the car you woke up and stuck your finger in your mouth and then I knew* Mum tells you again / *they had dug a body out of the rubble and could tell that it was Rozia by the dress* you say / *that's when I knew you would be my joy, because that's exactly what the child in my dream had done* she says and cries / *it happened a month or so after we'd left* / *at home your siblings gathered around the little bundle of you and sang* / *her face was blown off along with one arm* / *your brother had bought a tea set and your sister a ball almost as big as you were* / *no one looking at her could tell it was Rozia, they said* / *Gran had baked sweet bread and sewn a silk cap to shield you from the summer sun* / *I can't understand it* you say to the counsellor and shake your head / *the courtyard had been washed cool and clean, and for once the cat stayed away* / *I can't imagine not recognizing Rozia's face whatever it might look like* / *everyone was excited and I was ravenous* Mum says and laughs / do you think of her often, Marcus or Magnus asks softly / *we ate bean stew with rice and yoghurt and I drank a whole pot of tea afterwards* / you nod, of course you do / *Gran was the happiest of us all I think* / *I think of her and of my grandmother* you say and put the cup down / *she took you in her arms and then I made sure to sleep while I had the chance* / *do you know anything about black holes?* you later ask the counsellor / *and I only got out of bed the next morning, can you imagine?* / *inside a black hole is a place that is also a state—do you know about this?* you ask, facing Patrick or Henry in his chair / *a few days later Rozia's mother visited with little Rozia in her arms and a basket full of fruit* / no, I'm afraid I don't know much about space, says Eric or Martin and continues to take no notes / *then the two of you would meet up practically every day* / you say *it's called the singularity—that's what the place is called* and lean over the bed / *you and Rozia were like twins, we thought—the same round face and your hair as big and black* / *inside the singularity, the force of gravity is so strong it can't be calculated, can you imagine?* you tell the counsellor / *the pair of you often played in Rozia's yard and sometimes you stood by the big road even though you weren't allowed to and the soldiers could show up at any moment* / *that force pushes bodies together and renders the distance between them nil* / *because you both liked Gran's fried potatoes and her bean stew, you mostly ate at ours* Mum says / you use your hands to show how no space remains between bodies in the singularity / *she breastfed you once, Rozia's mother* / *eventually they occupy the same space* you say / *I was sick and my eye had started bleeding again, and then she came over with Rozia and fed you both* / *and if there's no distance between two bodies, it's pointless to go on talking about distance, right?* / *and when Gran and*

I had a lot to do, you and your siblings would sleep at theirs, do you remember that? / like the earth in a burial plot you say and press the button nearest the bed, wait for the nurse to turn up / *before we left, you gave my prettiest dress to Rozia even though I didn't want you to—do you remember that?* you ask Mum later as you sit on a bench outside the entrance to the hospital / *I'd like to have my lunch now* you say to the nurse when she appears in the doorway / *yes, I remember—you cried when you were looking through your bag and saw that it was missing, you wanted to go back* Mum says / *the fish please* you say *and some cordial too / you said she'd already been given a gift—your colouring book, isn't that right? / and after lunch, I just want to rest* / you nod—*yes, that's right, she got the one with a rabbit by a sunflower field at sunset* you say, *she liked that one* as you get up from the bench.

Day 3

Like every afternoon, the room is full of your loved ones, always nearby and always the first to meet the doctors you don't want to talk to / *Rozia, have you heard—the neighbour's cat was at our house again and now Mum is angry* / you stroke and stroke your belly and hope your body will hold / *I know—I told her it was the rooster who started it, but she's still angry* / you hear your brother crying and wonder how long he can sit here before they stop calling him in to work / *no, it's not possible, we can't go to the playhouse today, the cat broke a dish* / with them in the room, you allow yourself to do what you're longing to do, like giving your face a hard slap or pulling your hair, fistfuls of it in your lap / *we can go tomorrow—then we can bring meat and milk and cordial and sugar* / the doctors sometimes ask your siblings to talk some sense into you and when they come back into the room your siblings tell it like it is—what the doctors have asked of them / *Rozia, did you hear that my sister's school was bombed?* / someone says *what have we done wrong, God* and someone else *it will all work out, just calm down, trust in providence* /

well, yes, I swear—it happened last weekend, it's in ruins now / someone approaches you, it's your sister, she has just been sick / *no, no one died, but now there's almost nothing left of it* / she lifts your hand off your stomach and holds it, tells you that you're still young, that life is long and anything is possible / *now she just sits at home drawing and reading, can you imagine anything better?* / she tells you that you can have a big family if you want, that there's time for everything, that life goes on / *yes, but we're not even in school, Rozia* / outside you see another part of the hospital, count the storeys, ten in total / *Mum says that whatever the case, this isn't working anymore, we have to leave soon and we have to get out of here* / you have to get up there somehow, you know you do, it's all you want right now / *I don't know when, I've asked several times, but she isn't responding* / as high as you can get and then an open window—that's all / *no, not tomorrow, but maybe in a month or a year or so* / *can someone please tell the doctors that I want to get out of here* you say and look at your siblings / *I don't know, Rozia, she's not saying, can we please play instead?* / someone is crying loudly, you can't see who, you don't care / *behind the house, I think—bring the hand puppet with you and come* you say and run to the back.

Day 4

Again the counsellor is sitting across from you, asking you to explain your thinking / the day before you leave, Mum doesn't mention anything / why don't you want to birth your child? / she simply asks if you want to give Rozia a present because it's Best Friends Day today and then points to the calendar where she's scribbled something down / what do you think will happen if you keep the child in your belly? / you take out the colouring book with the rabbit and the sunflower field and wrap it up in newspaper / what do you hope to avoid by not taking that pill? / Gran wraps a yellow silk ribbon around it and now the package looks complete / what will happen to the child if it's kept inside? / when you bring it over to Rozia's, she says she has a package too, that her mother told her about Best Friends Day and she's ready for it / how will life proceed with the child in there? / it's a sparkly cloth bag containing Rozia's prettiest hair clip / is there something about what you're doing that you feel is bringing you closer to the child—is that why you're doing this? / you've wished for one just like this, begged and begged and said you want to be as pretty as Rozia, that it's not fair / if the child leaves you physically, does that make it any less yours? / Rozia helps you fix the hair clip to your bangs and then says *it's really nice on you* / will you feel more alone after it leaves you? / Mum wakes you up at dawn, says it's time, that you need to get dressed / most people in this situation have a different reaction / *I haven't finished packing* you say and Mum replies that she's packed the last of it for you, that she's been up all night, that all the important things are there / most people want to birth their babies as soon as possible, the counsellor says and tells you about these other people / *what about Rozia, I have to say goodbye to Rozia, I promised* / they feel that giving birth marks an important step forward / *if you hurry, you can draw a picture—Rozia's mother is sitting in the kitchen, she can take it with her* Mum says and goes down the stairs / the grief lasts forever but rituals have meaning / before you get in the car Rozia's mum kisses you on the cheek, says she'll miss you, that you'll see each other again soon, that they'll catch up with you on the other side of the border / because of the birth and then a burial ceremony of some kind, most people feel they can move on / *as we drove away I turned and looked back at the house, the balcony, the palms and at Rozia's mother who was waving and sprinkling a glass of water behind us, but I don't know if I looked long enough* Mum says later / how do you feel, don't you want to move past this? / *afterwards I always felt like I didn't look long enough* / this situation is of course physically untenable, even you know that / *it's always felt like I was never quite ready* Mum says / so what's the point of holding on to it? the counsellor says and looks at you.

You sit up in bed, take a look around, adjust your shirt and the sheet covering the bed.

When you put it like that you say to the counsellor afterwards *you're revealing everything you can't comprehend / first we went to an abandoned house and then to a tent camp in the desert* Mum says / *what do you think a child is—replaceable? / Gran started having regrets and said she wanted to be left behind, that she'd rather live among these rocks and mountains than elsewhere, and that she would rather be hiding in her own country than fleeing / when you talk about rituals—do you mean the one where you have to abandon your home? / she said there was no separating life and land and language and children, but we couldn’t just leave her there* Mum says / *when you talk about keeping something—do you mean the mother tongue that isn’t allowed to be spoken? / in the tents we lay on blankets, all except you and Gran / when you talk about moving past this—do you mean from exile? / you two slept on the only mattress we were given and I took the only pillow / when you speak of a normal reaction—do you mean to the knowledge of all those who have disappeared? / your sister got her period during this time, we didn’t know how to keep her dry, where to wash ourselves / when you talk about loneliness—do you mean my mother who sits alone all day in her rented one-bedroom outside the city? / during the day the sun was unbearable and during the night we were freezing cold / when you talk about burial ceremonies—do you mean the one for my grandmother, who is lying at one end of the cemetery out here? / the first few days, Gran sat outside the tent most of the time / it’s dishonest to talk about grief when you know nothing about it, wouldn’t you agree? / she didn’t want to talk, not even with you, and when I brought her tea, she asked me to pour it back and when I brought her bread, she didn’t want it / this isn’t temporary* you say / *the night before we and two other families were to meet up with the smugglers a few miles away, I let her commune with the earth awhile, made space for her to lie down and cover herself with it if she so wanted / I don’t understand what I’m supposed to be moving past* you say, facing the window / *cover yourself in your earth, in life if not in death, I said to her and told her that later I would heat water and wash the earth off her myself, use that soap we’d been given, take my time and be thorough / I don’t understand what constitutes forward movement or even what forward is / she came in after only an hour and said it didn’t matter how long she communed with the earth—if she wasn’t allowed to stay with it, no amount of time would be enough / can traumas be ranked?* you ask after a while / *later I saw that she had filled a handkerchief with earth and put it in her bag / I remember crying when I first saw this country / once we’d made it here you asked for Rozia every day, wondering if we were going to pick her up at the train station, if now was when she’d be arriving / it was February and wet, can you imagine anything worse / you dreamed about her, cried in your sleep, woke up tired and fretful / I told Mum I wanted to go back, that I wanted to be with Rozia, but that wasn’t possible / at the time I didn’t know that they were no longer alive* Mum says and stamps her feet in the snow / *at the refugee unit we were given cornflakes and hard bread for breakfast and sometimes a bit of salted cod roe, I retched when I first tasted it / and then when I found out what had happened, I had no idea what to say / as well as milk and yellow cheese that gave us a stomach ache / there were so many people who disappeared then* Mum says quietly / *the room was so small, two bunk beds and an extra mattress that my brother put next to the wall / Gran's cousin and my paternal aunt's entire family and my childhood friend Leyli along with her husband and children—do you remember them? / in the preparation course, the teacher laughed at my pronunciation once / still it was hardest to hear about Rozia / I was only seven years old and already spoke two languages, but she was laughing, the bitch / it was so strange too, because when I heard about what had happened to Rozia, I came to think of our house / today I'd probably have slammed that mouth of hers into her desk / if their house had been bombed, then our house was also in ruins / yes—I'd have slammed that mouth of hers right into her desk if she laughed at my child's pronunciation* you say and put a hand on your unmoving belly / *and in my memory that house is indestructible, do you know what I mean?* Mum says and looks at you under your dark beanie in the hospital grounds nearest the entrance.

On the walk back, you and Mum talk about what she did with the plush rabbit you bought on that final occasion and whether she should bring other clothes now that you're going to be here a while.

Yes, another sweater and pants you say—*and more underwear in case I bleed through.*

You ask her to bring the rabbit—saying you want to put it on the windowsill—and also the picture of the girl, the one you've been keeping in your notebook, which still smells of the soap you stashed away.

Do you know which one I mean? you ask Mum and she nods, *the girl on the corniche* she says and you correct her, say *the mother on the corniche—with the photo of her girl in her bag* and Mum nods yet again.

Just bring the notebook on the kitchen table and my good black pen you say and get up, kick the snow off your boots and go past reception back to the hospital room.

THE LOSSES

You sit down at a café in the galleria, pick up your notebook and your good black pen. From here you have a good view of the people moving along walkways, in and out of the shops. Once you've sat here awhile, you notice a man, it's the third time he has walked past you. He has a rosary in his hand and the same pants as Rozia's dad and all the other men from your childhood. You realize this is how he spends his day when it's raining or snowing—walking round and round the galleria closest to his home.

The train is heading north, stopping everywhere, picking up more and more people the closer to the big city you come. When you all finally arrive, it's snowing and it's wet, night even though it's only four o'clock. Your mother has lost track of the other families you were travelling with, doesn't know when they got off, thought you were all going to the same city. You and your siblings keep asking where you're going and what you're going to do next—turning to Mum just like you used to do at home—but unlike then Mum simply answers *I don't know* or *I don't understand*, says *I can't make sense of these signs* and then *wait a minute, I'll see.* Not until Gran exhausted sits down on the shiny floor of the station building and some guards approach her to ask her to stand up does Mum manage to get out some of the words she has memorized. She says that she's a political refugee and this is her family, that she has been fleeing for months trying to reach this place and now she wants to seek asylum here. You pick up your bags and follow the guards into a room.

What sort of place is this? your sister says the first time you step through the doors of the refugee reception unit and see a large foyer with mirrors and a painting, a fringed green rug with a floral pattern, and a little farther on a sign pointing out the toilets. By the stairs are other families, who like you are waiting with their bags in a cluster, and in the distance a blond woman and a man are going through documents. Later your sister finds out that this was a conference hotel and it's near to where she lives now, she can walk right over and have a look if she likes. *I would never do that* she says as the two of you sit at the kitchen table, drinking your afternoon tea. *I've considered it* you say and look out—*but only so as to write about it one day* and then remember the dining room and the laundry room, the grocery store, the motorway and the white girl who'd come by during the week to play while her parents, the owners of the facility, sat in their office.

Gran doesn't dare ride the elevator up to the little room you've been issued and says *we should always stick together* as she's getting dizzy on the big spiral staircase with the fringed floral rug. That night after dinner, you ride with her in the elevator up to the door of your shared room—*just so she doesn't get lost or stuck somewhere* Mum says softly and from then on this is your job. Sometimes you don't say a word until you're outside the door to the room, but for the most part you talk about how bad those fish balls and potatoes tasted, that tomorrow it'll have to be hard bread instead, how it scarcely matters anymore that it makes you sick to the stomach.

Every day your mum asks you kids to buy bread or milk and in this way gets you to go out awhile. *But not after four o'clock* she says one afternoon when you've suggested going to the grocery store to buy some soft drinks and a sponge cake. *But it's light out now, Mum* your brother says and points to the April sun outside—*and besides it might not have been racists who beat Hamid up, we talked yesterday and he said he didn't see who they were, after all they came from behind* he says. *Even so* Mum says, sitting on the bottom bunk with a pen and paper and a dictionary in hand—*I want you all home by four.*

So you weren't born here? they ask during the third and final interview for the job you would very much like to have. *No, I came here when I was six years old* you say and fall silent. You know what's going on, where the woman who asked the question is going with this. It's very impressive, says the man who might become your boss, that you know so many languages and have managed so well, he says. On the way out of the interview he'll tell you that the office has planned a business trip, that your language skills would be a perfect fit for the trip to the city with the corniche, that they'll bear this in mind as they review the final candidates.

The caseworker will pick you all up from the refugee unit, give you train tickets and the document that includes a map and directions to the house where you will be living. *Does it have a garden* Gran asks—*can you ask her if the house has a garden* she asks turning to your sister and your sister asks the caseworker about it, speaks well, has taught herself just by watching TV and reading books at the library closest to the refugee unit. The caseworker says that the house has a small garden, yes, but the accommodation is temporary, which you must bear in mind. *That's all I need* Gran says—*I simply want to rest my hands in the earth a while* she says, facing the caseworker, who does not understand.

The first night in the house you all stay up late, eating and drinking what little you brought with you. Mum lays out a blanket on the living room floor and sets out white cheese, bread and tea on the oven tray she found. *Isn't it lovely* Mum then says—*to be sitting here like we used to at home* and looks outside at the summer evening.

That summer the five of you take long walks through the neighbourhood and down to the lake. *None of us should have to ask anyone for directions* Mum says, leading you down the pavement—*in this country, you have to make your own way and that's precisely what we're going to do* she says and takes a turn that leads to what will soon be your school.

It's when you pronounce the word *went* that the teacher in the preparation course starts laughing. It's a W sound, not a V, she says and draws all the children along with her. It's your first day of school and Mum has plaited your hair shiny and tied it with bows that she had sewn from a shawl the night before. Later you don't want to go to school, saying you don't like that teacher and you want to go back to your real home, back to Rozia.

One evening Gran tries to bake sweet bread for you, to cheer you up. *I can't get my head around these ovens—ours were much faster and better* she says, turning the knobs on the oven this way and that. Then when she opens the bag of flour, she notices that it's brown. *The flour, it's brown* she calls out to Mum. *Then I've made a mistake* Mum says and picks up the bag, tries to read it. *It does say flour* she says turning it around—*isn't this flour?* and shows your brother who's now standing next to her. *Yes, but it says garham up here* he says. *No, it doesn't* says your sister, who has set her library book aside and stood up from her chair. *It says graham* she says, pointing. *Oh, well yes it does* Mum says and kisses you as you wait by the oven. *Just double the sugar and it'll be fine.*

You come home with the school's new weekly newsletter, give it to Mum. She calls to your sister and brother, asks them to read it as well, takes out the dictionary and a notebook. You ask if you can watch TV in the meantime and she says it's fine, you can watch until bedtime.

Neither your sister nor your brother have to take a preparation course, *there are no teachers for what this is*, Mum says as she straightens the collars of their jackets and tosses a glass of water behind them as they go. When the homeroom teacher sees your brother sitting there among the other children in the room to which he has been directed, he comes over, asks, so who do we have here? Then he gives a mild laugh, says that there must have been a mistake, that he'll accompany your brother to the principal's office, who in turn can point him in the right direction. When they return from their visit to the principal, the homeroom teacher doesn't say a word, shows your brother to where he was sitting just a moment before and asks the students to turn to chapter five.

Early in the morning when your mum leaves for her language course on the other side of the city, it falls to your sister to plait your hair. She tugs at it and doesn't brush it out properly, uses rubber bands instead of bows and leaves you with flyaways. Then she has to help you with your jacket, roll up your pants, make sure you have your PE bag. When that's done, she sits down in the hall, puts her head in her hands. *Did we leave everything behind just so I could help some snot-nosed kid with stuff she should be able to do herself?* she screams. You're still standing there, waiting for her to take you to school.

On Saturday afternoons you and your siblings usually play soccer in the schoolyard nearest the house. Sometimes other children pass by, but none want to play when you all are there. Gran and Mum usually take a seat on the bench opposite, pour tea from the thermos and place sugar cubes on their tongues. *What do you think of the earth in the yard* Mum asks—*do you think anything can grow there?* Gran straightens her headscarf, waves as if to chase away a fly. *I've put my hands in the earth several times* she says—*but I don't feel anything. This has never happened to me before* Gran says and puts the tea to her lips—*the earth not speaking to me.*

You call your mother to tell her that you got the job, that they've finally called with the news, that you start in two weeks. *Cordial and sugar* she cheers into the phone—*date cakes and incense* she says and asks you to come home immediately. *Since you'll be quitting that awful hourly job anyway* she adds and you say you'll miss your co-workers but certainly not the warehouse.

It's your first winter in the house with the little garden, the darkness outside. Something hard hits the windows and your brother stands up, puts on his coat. After a while he comes back in, says he needs something to wipe off the dog shit from the window and the mailbox. In his hand is a blue-and-yellow sticker that he's torn off, like the ones you've seen high up on lampposts around town.

The first time you correct your mother's pronunciation in front of your white schoolmates, she speaks up, asks you to stop, reminds you that she can talk however she likes as long as she makes herself understood. You don't understand why she's angry, you just want her to learn and so you keep correcting her. After a while she doesn't speak up anymore and instead starts talking about herself as being bad at the language, saying it like a joke at the start of every conversation with white people, that she talks a little funny and they should excuse her.

In the morning, right as your brother is changing after PE, his schoolmate yells that the locker room stinks of kebab sweat and eyes him. Do you always have to wear that same shirt, he says before he disappears—it's ugly and rank and you look like a girl. Your brother is heading to woodworking two buildings away and the jacket Mum found at the secondhand shop doesn't keep him warm as he runs across the schoolyard.

So there you are again, Gran you say when you get home from school and see her sitting by the kitchen window next to the radiator. She hugs you, says she's managed to vacuum and mop too, but that the days are so long here and there's nothing on TV. *How many people have you seen go by then?* you say, brushing the snow from your bangs. *Three* Gran says and pours tea to warm you both up.

In class everyone talks about Christmas, how wonderful it is, how you have to have a Christmas tree, don't you have one? *We celebrate our own holidays* Mum says when you complain *and besides, we can't afford it right now.* Nonetheless during the end-of-year sale she buys the loveliest Christmas tree you've ever seen and then your brother drives it home in a shopping cart you borrow from the supermarket. When you meet up with a schoolmate on the first day of school to play in the snow, you tell her that you have a Christmas tree now too, it's really pretty and has a star on top. Hold on, she says—it's too late for that now, Christmas is over.

Later, your mum tells you that the first thing she was told after talking about how she had been tortured in prison was that no one would hire a person like her. One eye missing, older and not entirely fluent—it'll be tough, the caseworker had said.

Your new workplace has a beautiful façade, is centrally located. You get there at the stated time and ring the bell, are met by the assistant. *Am I the first one here today?* you ask and she laughs and says that you'll probably be the first one here every day if you arrive at this hour. Nine-thirty will do, she says, and shows you to your desk. Later when you all return from your trip, you decide to make the desk space more your own, put up a postcard with an old image of the mountains behind the corniche from back when the corniche was open to the sea, as well as a picture of you and your gran on a summer's day in the park.

You are ten years old the first time you scheme to get a notebook from the grocery store. Your family can't afford anything but food and to get it you say that the teacher asked you to bring one to school, that it's important, that everyone else has one but you and it's embarrassing. You say you need it the very next day and in the moment—among the shelves crowded with batteries and erasers, rolls of tape and wrapping paper—you are fully aware that Mum doesn't have the courage to call the school and check. Later, you set it aside, say it's for Rozia, that she can have it as soon as she arrives.

Your sister has walked all the way home in the rain. As soon as she throws off her outer layers, she says she needs a shower, goes into the bathroom, disappears. As you pass by, you hear her crying in there, tell Gran, say she seems really sad, that the two of you have to do something. Gran says to leave her be, that your sister is having a hard time right now, that she misses her friends like you miss Rozia.

My friends actually get some of their kiddie cash, you know you say to your brother as you're sitting around the kitchen table—he absorbed in a book and you with your sketchbook. *It's called child benefit, dummy, and I want you to stop talking about it—Mum barely has enough money for food* he says without looking up.

For the first five years after you left, you celebrate Rozia's birthday. You draw her a picture, which Mum puts in the mail, and then you eat chocolate pralines, her favourite. The next day you tell your schoolmate about the celebration and she responds by saying that she has a pen pal too, it's Lisa in the parallel class, they exchange letters during the breaks sometimes.

Later Mum asks if you'd like some Easter decorations and if she should gather some twigs on the way home for you both to tie some fabric to. *Isn't that the kind of thing your schoolmates do?* she repeats when you don't respond. *There's no need* you say after a while—*the Christmas tree was enough, thanks.*

You tell the office about your pregnancy, say that it's unexpected but welcome and that you are looking forward to experiencing what many before you have also experienced. Have you thought about a name? your co-worker asks—there are lots of trendy ones these days. You say you don't know, the only name that has come to mind is Rozia, who was your best friend. Does it come from the word for rose? he asks—is it the same in your language? *It is* you say *but this particular name comes from the word for day*. Ah-ha, he then says and laughs—Dayia.

The first time your grandmother finds out that the white schoolmates you're having over would rather eat pancakes than her stew, she doesn't understand. She stands at the stove happy to finally have a task, has already sliced the onions and potatoes, heated up the oil. *You and Rozia liked my food* she says quietly and you reply *I still do, Gran, but could you please make pancakes today?*

It's spring and at your brother's school everyone is talking about summer jobs. Your brother has applied for a dozen, doesn't know what more he can do. The competition is tough, his white schoolmate says as they walk down the corridor to the cafeteria. *So where are you working this summer?* my brother asks, and he replies, with Dad.

What do you have in mind for the future? your sister's teacher asks her at the end of the term. *I'd like to qualify for university* your sister says happily—*to study history or geography, I'm not quite sure.* Afterwards she tells you that her teacher said that was brave and ambitious, but perhaps she should consider becoming a day-care assistant instead, that she'd be well suited to it, since she's already so considerate.

One day the teacher thinks it's time for everybody to switch seats. She puts you next to the most popular girl in the class, who removes her hoodie and shows off the swastika she has carved into her forearm. When you tell the teacher about the swastika and ask for a different seat, she tells you that you're just kids and the girl will grow out of it soon. Besides, isn't it in fact a very good thing that she has the opportunity to sit next to you, since you can show her just how wrong she is about immigrants?

Later your mum gets a job as a middle school mother-tongue teacher and celebrates by buying you both ice cream. *It's only an hourly gig* she says *and I'm not working with high school students like back home, still it's something* she says and takes a bite of her cone. Before you leave the galleria, you persuade her to treat herself to a new shirt, saying she really can't use the one she has on anymore, the collar is in tatters.

Your new boss asks you what you think about the destination of the business trip. He says he knows the city has been ravaged by the war, but the architectural solutions are so fascinating. The fact that buildings covered in bullet holes have been left standing among newly built hotels and skyscrapers along the corniche—doesn't that just say everything about the world today? he says and looks at you. You reply that you find the trip problematic and that you don't see the development of the city in the same way, that much of what is considered a solution is mostly the result of a country in deep crisis and that it feels odd to study a place like that without a critical eye. What a shame, he then says. Unfortunately we can't change our destination at this stage, but perhaps you could compile a risk analysis for the trip? I think it might make everyone feel safer.

At your year-seven parent-teacher conference Mum shows up in the finest and most precious item she owns, a striped rabbit fur she received as a gift. A few year nines point at her and laugh, asking who the hell is that. Later on the walk home you take up a long lead, leaving her behind.

The first time your brother brings a white girl home, Mum and Gran cook up a storm, a proper feast of rice, salad and stews. Later they stop seeing each other. Your brother says her family was strange, he didn't like them and it's better this way. The third time things don't work out with a white girl he finally tells it like it is—her father didn't want her to be with an immigrant, and if she insisted upon it, she wouldn't get her share of her grandmother's inheritance.

Your sister moonlights as a day-care assistant, sometimes talking to the children in their shared language, laughing and joking around. At a weekly meeting, her co-worker asks if she has checked with the children's parents if it's okay—if she may speak a language other than the one spoken in this country, that is.

Sometimes when your schoolmates come over, Gran starts talking about Rozia. She does this after the friend has left, sees it as an opportunity to chat with you, thinks it will make you happy. Gran says *do you remember how you and Rozia used to swing in her garden?* or *do you remember the time you two wanted me to sew you each a cape?* For the most part you simply reply *yes* or *I remember* but on one occasion you get upset, say that your new friends are nothing like Rozia, that it's not the same thing, that it's boring when Gran only talks about what used to be.

Mum comes home and lies down on the sofa, falls asleep with her shoes on. Later she says that work wants her to expand her class, that more children have arrived who also need instruction in their mother tongue, that she has to take on another ten students.

You are sitting in the lunchroom at work, eating Mum's dolma out of the lunchbox she packed for you the day before. Is that the kind of thing we'll be eating on the corniche? your co-worker asks as she walks by—it smells divine. You say you don't know, you've never been to that country before.

You are sixteen years old when your gran tells you about her dead children, the one she lost after only a few months and Halima, who made it to five and loved cherries and had the silkiest hair on the block. *She fell ill after drinking from the well in the schoolyard* she says calmly when you ask—*that's how senseless death is* she says and takes you in her arms.

Hello, I am calling about my grandmother, she wants to make an appointment with a doctor to review her medication. . . . Yes, exactly, diabetes and high blood pressure. . . . Yes, she had that operation done in March of last year. . . . No, that's not necessary, I'll interpret.

It's Saturday night. You and your brother are telling each other about your days. You do it exclusively in the new language, fast and without pause, and Mum tries to follow. After a while she gets up from the sofa, switches the TV off, goes to bed.

You sit by your uncle's bedroll laid out on a rug during your first trip back. He is half-reclined, trying to reassure you that he wasn't always this worn out, telling you about how strong he was as a young man, that he'd work twelve hours straight carrying sacks back and forth across the market and that he did it every day. Between sentences he coughs, turning away so as not to bother you. Upon homecoming, you try to explain what you've experienced, how the house you so often visited as a child was unchanged, how there have never been sofas or beds there and how much you like that that's how it is. Your white friend looks at you and says that's great, even though she herself couldn't take it—if she so much as looks at a bedroll, she gets bruises.

At lunch your sister's co-worker asks if she was forced into her marriage. Well, I mean, I've read about how that kind of thing happens in your culture, she says—that you, as it were, don't get to choose. Later your sister says she'd wanted to ask if the woman's husband tends to travel overseas in order to buy children—*I've heard that happens in your culture, I wanted to say, but I couldn't* your sister tells you on the phone—*I can't afford to leave this job, plus I only have to see that racist hag twice a week so it's fine.*

Your gran talks about all the beautiful dresses she sewed in addition to the bedspreads and quilts, the curtains and tablecloths. She says *the women from the other side of town would see a dress on TV and bring it to me, ask me to sew one up for them, give me some fabric and some thread, and then it was done.* She talks about different styles and fabrics as the two of you walk around the clothing shop and the assistant eyeing you adjusts hangers that don't need adjusting.

The day before you go off on your business trip, Mum spends the night, tells you about everything you need to bear in mind, that you mustn't walk too much no matter how many buildings they want to study and that you must eat enough, drink enough, sleep well. *Don't buy too many books or earrings* she says as well as *don't sit in tobacco smoke, not even on the corniche.* You ask if she wants a souvenir from there and she says *absolutely not* and that's when you know exactly what to bring back for her.

The nurse who admits your mum asks your sister if it's essential that she accompany her—no need for a family reunion in the ER, she says, opening the door. *But I'm on my own* your sister says—*and she's my mother.*

Your brother has sent the manuscript of his novel to a publisher, is in high spirits as he talks about it. *They're into it* he says—*but they think it's too soft, that there's not enough of me in it or of today's harsh realities.* He plops down on the sofa next to you, puts his feet up just like you. *I don't understand* you say after a while—*do they want to know more about what it's like to be a physicist today?*

You go through a long period of unemployment and usually have no more than 700 kronor left after paying for a bus pass and all the bills. You meet your white friend at a café, reasoning that you can spend 30 kronor on a coffee if you sneak in some biscuits from home to eat on the sly. Your friend talks about her weekend, about her mother coming to visit, her vacant pied-à-terre. Your friend is considering moving in now that it's no longer a shared apartment, but thinks renting from her parents is a drag.

Your mum is sitting at the computer, trying to figure out what to do with the document she got from her employer. *Thank you for taking the time, darling* she says as you try to determine why she hasn't yet received the money for her sick leave. *The caseworker said I need to log in to My Pages* she says *but what do I do next?* and searches the screen.

Once you've landed in the city you tell your boss that you never imagined the mountains would be so big and so close. *And that the plane would fly right alongside them* you say *and that the corniche would be so bright!* Yes, your boss says proudly—isn't it fantastic?

None of your white friends have wanted to hear any of your memories from the war. It hits you one day as you're sitting with one of them, listening to him talk about how he used to pick berries with his grandmother as a child. He goes into minute detail, pulling out photos from when he was in the bilberry patch in the woods, one where he is sticking out his tongue, pulling a face. *Yes, but my friend Rozia was found in the rubble after a bombing, what do you think about that?* you say and wait for him to respond.

I'm hearing that you're functioning in your daily life, is that right? the psychiatrist asks your sister at the end of her assessment. *Well, yes, I am* your sister says—*but I have memories of the war that make me feel very bad, I need help dealing with them, it's having an impact on my children* she says. Later she begins again, calls the health centre, is again asked to describe her troubles.

Your gran's last wish is to not be buried in this earth, to be allowed to go back home. She says she should at least in death be allowed to rest in the arms of her ancestors—this is all she wants now, it is her only thought. Afterwards none of you know what to say.

Your brother and his friend argue about political consciousness. His friend says it's not his fault he grew up in a welfare state where neither he nor his parents had to take a major political stand. *The Vietnam War, apartheid, colonialism and segregation were also there for your parents to take a stand on* your brother says—*they just didn't give a shit, when are you going to see that?*

In the coffee shop at one end of the galleria, your mum is talking loudly on the phone about the validity of the independence referendum. A white woman stops demonstratively, watches her. *After a while I turned around and asked, what do you want?* Mum tells you on the phone when you call home from the hotel a few streets away from the corniche. *You have to understand that people like her are to be pitied* Mum says shortly afterwards—*their ignorance, how little they've experienced in life.* Later that same night you'll have dinner with your co-workers, and as soon as you've hung up, you take out your velvet dress, put your hair up. It's a spot the hotel recommended and is supposed to have a stunning view of the ocean and serve mostly organic produce from around the mountains, your boss tells you later as you're all walking up the long road, the sea and sky dark against the glittering corniche.

BALSAM KARAM (b. 1983) is of Kurdish ancestry and has lived in Sweden since she was a young child. She is an author, librarian and university lecturer, and made her literary debut in 2018 with the critically acclaimed *Event Horizon*, which was shortlisted for the Katapult Prize. *The Singularity* was shortlisted for the August Prize and is her first English-language publication.

SASKIA VOGEL is the author of *Permission* and the translator of over twenty Swedish-language books. She was awarded the Berlin Senate Endowment for Non-German Literature and was a finalist for the PEN Translation Prize. She worked on *The Singularity* as part of her translation residency at Princeton University. From Los Angeles, she now lives in Berlin.

More Translated Literature from the Feminist Press

The Age of Goodbyes by Li Zi Shu,
translated by YZ Chin

La Bastarda by Trifonia Melibea Obono,
translated by Lawrence Schimel

Blood Feast: The Complete Short Stories of Malika Moustadraf
translated by Alice Guthrie

Grieving: Dispatches from a Wounded Country
by Cristina Rivera Garza,
translated by Sarah Booker

Happy Stories, Mostly
by Norman Erikson Pasaribu,
translated by Tiffany Tsao

Human Sacrifices by María Fernanda Ampuero,
translated by Frances Riddle

In Case of Emergency by Mahsa Mohebali,
translated by Mariam Rahmani

The Living Days by Ananda Devi,
translated by Jeffrey Zuckerman

Panics by Barbara Molinard,
translated by Emma Ramadan

Sweetlust: Stories by Asja Bakić,
translated by Jennifer Zoble

Violets by Kyung-Sook Shin,
translated by Anton Hur

THE FEMINIST PRESS
AT THE CITY UNIVERSITY OF NEW YORK
FEMINISTPRESS.ORG